This is what happens

"An incisive reflection on how social forces constrain women's lives. … Great for fans of Sylvia Plath, Doris Lessing's *The Golden Notebook*." *Booklife*

"I find the writing style very appealing … An interesting mix of a memoir and a philosophical work, together with some amazing poetry. … This is what happens ranks in my top five of books ever read." Mesca Elin, *Psychochromatic Redemption*

Thus Saith Eve

"Short, but definitely entertaining … and serious between the lines." Lee Harmon, A Dubious Disciple Book Review

" … a truly wonderful source of feminist fiction. In addition to being an extremely enjoyable and thought-provoking read, the monologues can also be used for audition and performance pieces." Katie M. Deaver, feminismandreligion.com

Snow White Gets Her Say

"Why isn't anyone doing this on stage? … What a great night of theater that would be!" szferris, Librarything

"I loved the sassy voices in these stories, and the humor, even when making hard points." PJ O'Brien, Smashwords

Deare Sister

"You are clearly a writer of considerable talent, and your special ability to give expression to so many different characters, each in a uniquely appropriate style, makes your work fascinating and attractive. … The pieces are often funny, sometimes sensitive, always creative. But they contain an enormous load of anger, and that is where I have problems. … I know at least one feminist who would read your manuscript with delight (unfortunately she is not a publisher), who would roar with laughter in her sharing of your anger. …" rejection letter from Black Moss Press

Particivision and other stories

"... your writing is very accomplished. ... *Particivision and other stories* is authentic, well-written, and certainly publishable. ..." rejection letter from Turnstone Press

"... engaging and clever ..." rejection letter from Lester & Orpen Dennys, Publishers

"As the title indicates, this collection of stories is about getting into the thick of things, taking sides, taking action, and speaking out loud and clear, however unpopular your opinion may be. ... refreshingly out of the ordinary." Joan McGrath, *Canadian Book Review Annual*

dreaming of kaleidoscopes

"... a top pick of poetry and is very much worth considering. ..." *Midwest Book Review*

Soliloquies: the lady doth indeed protest

"... not only dynamic, imaginative verse writing, but extremely intelligent and intuitive insight. ... I know many actresses who would love to get their hands on this material!" Joanne Zipay, Judith Shakespeare Company, NYC

"'Ophelia' is something of an oddity ... I found it curiously attractive." *Dinosaur*

UnMythed

"... A welcome relief from the usual male emphasis in this area. There is anger and truth here, not to mention courage." Eric Folsom, *Next Exit*

"... With considerable skill and much care, chris wind has extrapolated truths from mythical scenarios and reordered them in modern terms. ... Wind handles these myths with and intellect. Her voice suggests that the relationship between the consciousness of the myth-makers and modern consciousness is closer than we would think." Linda Manning, *Quarry*

"Personally, I would not publish this stuff. This is not to say it isn't publishable—it's almost flawless stylistically, perfect form and content, etc., etc. It's perverse: satirical, biting, caustic, funny. Also cruel, beyond bitter, single-minded with a terminally limited point of view, and this individual may have read Edith Hamilton's *Mythology* but she/he certainly doesn't perceive the essential meanings of these myths. Or maybe does and deliberately twists the meaning to suit the poem. Likewise, in the etymological sense. Editorial revisions suggested? None, it's perfect. Market potential/readership targets: Everyone—this is actually marketable—you could sell fill Harbourfront reading this probably. General comments: You could actually make money on this stuff." anonymous reader report for a press that rejected the ms

Satellites Out of Orbit

"*Satellites Out of Orbit* is an excellent and much recommended pick for unique fiction collections." Michael Dunford, *Midwest Book Review*

"... I also love the idea of telling the story from the woman's perspective, especially when the woman is only mentioned in passing in the official story, or not mentioned at all. ..." Shana, Tales of Minor Interest

"Our editorial board loved it. Our readers said it was the most feminist thing they've read in a long time." rejection letter from publisher

As I the Shards Examine / Not Such Stuff

"*Not Such Stuff* challenges us to rethink some of our responses to Shakespeare's plays and opens up new ways of experiencing them. ... " Jeff, secondat.blogspot.com

"This world premiere collection of monologs derive from eight female Shakespearian characters speaking from their hearts, describing aspects of their lives with a modern feminist sensibility. Deconstructing the traditional interpretations of some of the most fiercely fascinating female characters of all time, the playwright is able to "have at it" and the characters finally have their say. And oh, what tales they have to weave. ..." Debbie Jackson, dctheatrescene.com

Let Me Entertain You

"I found this to be very powerful and visually theatrical." Ines Buchli

"I will never forget 'Let Me Entertain You.' It was brilliant." Kate Hurman

ProVocative

"Timely, thought-provoking, dark, and funny!" Kevin Holm-Hudson, WEFT

"… a great job making a point while being entertaining and interesting. … Overall this is a fine work, and worth listening to." Kevin Slick, *gajoob*

The Art of Juxtaposition

"A cross between poetry, performance art, and gripping, theatrical sound collages. … One of the most powerful pieces on the tape is 'Let Me Entertain You.' I sat stunned while listening to this composition." Myke Dyer, *Nerve*

"We found [this to be] unique, brilliant, and definitely not 'Canadian'. … We were more than impressed with the material. *The Art of Juxtaposition* is filling one of the emptier spaces in the music world with creative and intelligent music-art." rejection letter from a record company

"Controversial feminist content. You will not be unmoved." Bret Hart, *Option*

"I've just had a disturbing experience: I listened to *The Art of Juxtaposition*. Now wait a minute; Canadian musicians are not supposed to be politically aware or delve into questions regarding sexual relationships, religion, and/or sex, racism, rape. They are supposed to write nice songs that people can tap their feet to and mindlessly inebriate themselves to. You expect me to play this on my show?" Travis B., CITR

"Wind mixes biting commentary, poignant insight and dark humor while unflinchingly tackling themes such as rape, marriage (as slavery), christianity, censorship, homosexuality, the state of native Americans, and other themes, leaving no doubt about her own strong convictions upon each of these subjects. Her technique is often one in which two or more sides to each theme are juxtaposed against one another (hence, the tape's title). This is much like her *Christmas Album* with a voice just as direct and pointed. Highly recommended." Bryan Baker *gajoob*

"Thanks for *The Art of Juxtaposition* … it really is quite a gem! Last Xmas season, after we aired 'Ave Maria' a listener stopped driving his car and phoned us from a pay phone to inquire and express delight." John Aho, CJAM

"Liked *The Art of Juxtaposition* a lot, especially the feminist critiques of the bible. I had calls from listeners both times I played 'Ave Maria.'" Bill Hsu, WEFT

"Every time I play *The Art of Juxtaposition* (several times by this point), someone calls to ask about it/you." Mars Bell, WCSB

"The work is stimulating, well-constructed, and politically apt with regard to sexual politics. (I was particularly impressed by 'I am Eve.')" Andreas Brecht Ua'Siaghail, CKCU

"We have found *The Art of Juxtaposition* to be quite imaginative and effective. When I first played it, I did not have time to listen to it before I had to be on air. When I aired it, I was transfixed by the power of it. When I had to go on mike afterward, I found I could hardly speak! To say the least, I found your work quite a refreshing change from all the fluff of commercial musicians who whine about lost love etc. Your work is intuitive, sensitive, and significant!" Erika Schengili, CFRC

"Interesting stuff here! Actually this has very little music, but it has sound bits and spoken work. Self-declared 'collage pieces of social commentary'. …very thought-provoking and inspiring." *No Sanctuary*

more at
chriswind.net
and
chriswind.com

by chris wind

prose
This is what happens
Thus Saith Eve
Snow White Gets Her Say
Deare Sister
Particivision and other stories

poetry
dreaming of kaleidoscopes
Soliloquies: the lady doth indeed protest
UnMythed
Paintings and Sculptures

mixed genre
Satellites Out of Orbit
Excerpts

stageplays
As I the Shards Examine / Not Such Stuff
The Ladies' Auxiliary
Snow White Gets Her Say
The Dialogue
Amelia's Nocturne

performance pieces
I am Eve
Let Me Entertain You

audio work
ProVocative
The Art of Juxtaposition

Excerpts

chris wind

Magenta

Excerpts: miscellaneous prose and poetry
2nd Edition
© 1991, 2022 by chris wind

www.chriswind.net
www.chriswind.com

ISBN 978-1-926891-92-7 paperback
ISBN 978-1-926891-93-4 epub
ISBN 978-1-926891-94-1 pdf

Published by Magenta

Magenta

This is a work of fiction. Names, characters, places, brands, media, and incidents are either the product of the author's imagination or are used fictitiously. The author acknowledges the trademarked status and trademark owners of various products referenced in this work of fiction, which have been used without permission. The publication/use of these trademarks is not authorized, associated with, or sponsored by the trademark owners.

Cover design by chris wind
Formatting and interior book design by Elizabeth Beeton

Library and Archives Canada Cataloguing in Publication

Title: Excerpts : miscellaneous prose and poetry / Chris Wind.
Other titles: Works. Selections
Names: wind, chris, author.
Description: 2nd edition. | Previously published: Sundridge, Ontario : Magenta, 1991.
Identifiers: Canadiana (print) 20210143231 | Canadiana (ebook) 20210144610 |
    ISBN 9781926891927 (softcover) | ISBN 9781926891934 (EPUB) |
    ISBN 9781926891941 (PDF)
Classification: LCC PS8595.I592 A6 2022 | DDC C811/.54—dc23

Acknowledgements

"Two O'Clock Pick-Up" *Going for Coffee*, Tom Wayman, ed. (1980)

"tears erode" *Whetstone* (Spring 82)

"aria for solo flute" *Whetstone* (Spr83)

"Double Exposure" *event* 12.2 (Nov83)

"Faith" *The New Quarterly* IV.1 (Spring 84)

"This is the person" Ouroboros (1985)

"running" *Herizons* 3.5 (Jul/Aug85)

"Nocturne" *Hysteria* IV.4 (Spring 86)

"Show and Tell" *Waves* 15.1/2 (Fall 86)

"the apple" *Clever Cats* (Mar87)

"Of Human Bondage" *Poetry Toronto* 146 (Feb88)

"Adam's Apple" *grain* XVII.3 (Fall 89)

"suspended" *Canadian Woman Studies* 10.1 (Apr89)

"While i ..." *Kola* 8.1 (1995)

Preface to second edition

Initially, I was tempted to dismiss *Excerpts* as juvenilia and, therefore, leave it as a first edition print-only collection, of relevance only to those interested in roots. But "Adam's Apple" (along with a few other pieces) changed my mind (and so I prepared this slightly revised edition for ebook and print-on-demand distribution, enabling greater presence and availability). I recall standing outside on the sidewalk after viewing Judy Chicago's *The Dinner Party* and just ... crying; my soon-to-be ex-boyfriend said he didn't see what I was so upset about. I wrote "Adam's Apple" soon after. In hope, perhaps. (Though, thirty-five years later, I'd add to the short list in the poem more references to the oppression, and suppression, of women. Hundreds, thousands, more.)

Contents

Faith

She woke in sudden, sharp perplexity.

Glancing beside, three o'clock, she—she was hot and sweaty. Shamed, guilty, she lifted herself from the bed, careful not to disturb her husband's sleep, and knelt on the cold rug. *Forgive-me-Father-for-I-have-not-sinned*—she looked up in abrupt remembrance—*it was* not *that kind of dream. There was a word.* She knelt back on her heels. *But why so clammy and tensed, what was the word?* Exasperated at the typical elusiveness of a thing intentionally sought, she rose and went to the bathroom to rinse her face. She climbed back into bed. *Maybe in the morn—test. That's it. The word was* test. *That's stupid. I'm not going to write any tests.* At three-o-five it didn't matter. She fell asleep.

The alarm rudely buzzed. She reached out to—*test of fate.* The phrase appeared serenely. *Was that it? Test of fate? Yes, I think so. Well isn't that curious. Test of fate.*

"Hey Kath—the alarm." He looked at her drugged expression. "The alarm. Turn it off. Turn off the alarm." His words finally made their way through, and she turned off the alarm.

"Good morning to you, too." She leaned over and kissed his bemused mouth.

Just then the sound of tiny, pyjama-clad feet down the hall announced the little boy's cheerful face at their doorway.

"Good morning to you, too," he imitated, and giggled. Then the sight of his mother seemed to trigger—he looked down and mumbled, "Mummy-I-wet-my-bed-I'm-sorry."

"That's okay, snookums." Resisting the smile that snuck to her lips, she added in a stern voice, "If you help me clean it up." Then she smiled anyway, "Let's go." She and the boy left the room hand in hand.

"… which we are about to receive from Thy bounty, through Christ our Lord, Amen." The bowed heads had just enough time to chorus the "Amen" before the littlest one bobbed up and declared, "Mummy 'n I are going shopping for my new school clothes and I'm getting new school shoes and she says I can pick them out if I can put them on by myself and we're going to buy a pencil case I want a red one—"

"Hold it there, shooter," laughed his father. "So you're getting ready for school. Think you'll like it?"

"Yeah, Mummy says there'll be other kids there, too."

"Joey, you'll have eggs instead of words coming out of that mouth of yours in a minute if you don't watch it." She smiled at the boy, then looked over to her husband. "Don't forget I have the Scripture Group tonight."

"Right. Got your notes prepared?"

"Oh sure. But it's a good class. They carry it quite well without my notes. I need only ask the right questions at the right time."

"Hm—sometimes difficult." He kept on chewing.

"True. But I know what I'm doing." She was irritated. He was still unconvinced that a woman could do as well as a man in the matter of adult religious instruction. *Chauvinist! Conditioning or no conditioning, there's no excuse. Oh well. He'll see eventually. That's all. I'm strong, capable, intelligent. He'll have to see.* She cleared the breakfast table and started the dishes as he said his goodbyes to Joey and left for the office.

Test…test of… fate…test…….kill Ty….test…kill… Kathy snapped up in the darkness, and as soon as she did, the words stopped. She was very hot again. *Or is it the room that's hot?* She tried to recall the superstition about having the same dream twice in a row. *Same dream— who are you trying to kid. That was no dream. You know you heard words. Well, some dreams can be that real, can't they? But somebody was speaking.* She cautiously got up to see if the windows were open. Feeling foolish, she returned to bed.

She stopped her car at another red light. Noting her watch, she realized she was a few minutes late tonight. *I shouldn't have let Joey model his new clothes again, she chuckled. That little guy. Such a ham already. That's one very eager student coming—kindergarten class, make way!* Suddenly the car became quite warm. Automatically she looked at the indicators. All was normal. *Test...test...kill Ty...test......kill Tyson...Tyson...* A honk jarred her from the daze and cut off the words. Eventually she noticed the green light and put her foot to the gas. *Kill Tyson? Who's Tyson? Was that what was said?* Then it occurred to her. *Two nights, okay, dreams—but in the evening on the way to church? Test of fate. Kill Tyson. What the heck does that mean?* It made no sense to her. *Okay. If it happens again tonight, I'll just lie 'here, hear it out instead of getting up, startled. Maybe that'll do it.*

Kathy lay in bed anxiously, expectantly. *This is absurd.* But she was sure. *I am not imagining.* Even so, she reconsidered. *Here I am, lying in bed waiting for something to speak--anything else go bump in the night?* She rolled over. *Test...test of...Stay put don't move a muscle. Test...test...* The room became hot. *Of faith... as test of faith—faith, not fate, the word was—test of faith...kill.* She was trembling now, trying desperately to hang on to her calm. *Faith...kill...* The words were very clear now, she noticed...*of faith...kill...thy son—Oh my God.* In a spasm of shock she bumped the alarm to the floor and kicked her husband. The words were gone. She was shivering. *Oh God.* She felt the soaked bed with shaking hands and started towards the bathroom. Suddenly she turned and half ran to Joey's room. He was asleep in bed and breathing normally. *The voice was distinct and I was awake all the time.* She sat down in the chair beside his bed and dropped exhausted into a deep sleep.

Her husband looked at her from across the breakfast table. Then he looked out to Joey in the backyard. He turned back to her, having heard everything she had just told him, and simply said, "Well, I don't think there's a need to be upset, dear. I mean, it was just a dream." He paused, searching for a way to reason or reassure. "All the tensions—the Scripture Group and—you know. They all get into your sleep," he ended lamely. Then continued with a little impatience. "You studied Freud. Doesn't he call dreaming a release outlet or something?"

She turned away. He didn't believe her. He just didn't believe her. Her husband, joined with her in the sacrament of matrimony in the sight of God, dismissed these words of His as a Freudian twist. She told him she was terrified and ashamed of the fear, and he thought it was nothing to get upset about. She got up and stood by the window. *Scripture Group, my foot.* She turned to see him pick up the paper again. *I feel no tension from them.*

"Yes, Kathy, come right in. How are you, and how is the Scripture Group coming? I've been wanting to speak with you."

She stepped through the doorway into the rectory. "Hello, Father. I'm fine, thank you, and you?"

"Oh, I'm fine, too. The Council has okayed the new addition and the youth choir is on its way. Now tell me, how is that group?" The priest led her into his study and motioned to a chair.

"Oh, it's doing very well." She sat down. "I was just telling Peter, they do most of the talking. It's turned out to be quite a lively bunch. As a matter of fact, in a way, that's why I'm here—"

"Oh, too lively for you?" The priest smiled.

'Too lively for me?" She was on the defensive. "Father, you recall—" before she saw the twinkle in his eye. She laughed and returned the rib. "I was baptised by you. How can anything be too tough for me?" Without allowing a retaliation, she leaned forward and went on. "But tell me, what does the doctor of divinity"—the priest smiled at this nickname—"say about contradictory principles in the Bible?"

"Oh, you've opened up a mean can of worms with that one, Kathy. Give me a 'for instance'."

"Well, the commandment 'Thou shalt not kill' and the so-called 'Holy Wars'. The commandments were given by God, were they not? And as such, the absolute word of God. Yet he more or less blessed those murders, didn't he?"

At first the priest was angry. "You're asking me to justify the ways of God to man?"

"I suppose I am," she replied. But she saw nothing wrong with that. "Are they unjustifiable? Do we not deserve an explanation?"

"We don't deserve anything from God!"

"Surely—"

The priest held up his hand, then paused before he replied. "God does have mysteries—fantastic mysteries—that we cannot begin to understand. We must be strong and have faith. We *must* believe that whatever, *whatever*"—he stressed the magnitude of the word—"*God's* will be done. You know," he chuckled now, "the Lord works in wondrous ways."

Kathy looked at him. Suppressing her disappointment, she exchanged a few more pleasantries with the priest then left the rectory.

She went directly to the church. After passing through the expansive mahogany doors and blessing herself with the holy water in the marble font, she entered the nave, genuflected, and slumped into the second last pew. She stared for a moment at the crucifix, high on the wall behind the altar, then began.

Okay, let's take Freud a bit further. Could it be more than tension? Could it be a murmur, a message of sorts, from my subconscious?

She answered the question as quickly as it had formed. *Nonsense. I don't have any hidden desire to kill my—to kill Joey. To even think it horrifies me. He's my son, my flesh and blood. I carried him, gave birth to him, almost lost— no God let me, let him, gave him my milk, he's—* She started sobbing, cries in a silence.

She made another attempt to order the chaos. *As a test of faith, kill thy son. I'm sure I heard those words. Distinctly. Clearly.*

Sure, you may believe you heard them.

No, I know.

What's the difference? Something tottered precariously. *I mean, are you the seat of objective knowledge? Don't presume. Kath—*

But—

You hear what you want to hear. Face it. You interpret how you want to understand. Shall we then perhaps contemplate the sin of pride instead of murder?

Oh come on—

Surely you don't really think yourself pure enough to be selected, chosen by God for this special test?

She felt a brick fall from the wall inside. It was a long way.

Okay, if I'm not chosen, then I'm wrong even to assume the words were spoken by God!

My point exactly. That was your imposed interpretation.

But if the devil or some evil entity issued them, why say as a 'test of faith'?

Well, my dear, do you really think he's going to expose himself? That would defeat his purpose. Do you think he's stupid?

But if he can deceive me into believing he's the voice of God, what chance do I stand? How do I know?

The very mortar seemed to be melting … *lead us not into temptation …*

Okay if it happened at all—

You're saying if. Would you kill your son on an 'if'?

Of course not. I'm his mother. I—

But isn't that what faith is—an 'if'?

Yes. No. I know God exists. I know that He—

Do you?

Oh God! How can I be sure? Give me a sign—

Oh come on, Kathy. What more of a sign do you need? Three consecutive nights and once on King Street before nightfall. That's no coincidence.

But it's no proof, either. Was she on the other side of the wall now? How—

But the heat. Every time He was present—

You were hot. The flushes come and go. You can't deny that. It's a normal occurrence in your life now—

But—

If the heat meant anything, it meant temporary delirium.

The wall began to sway.

As a test of faith, kill thy son. Why am I trying to escape this? If I were strong in my faith, I—

But it's such a clumsy way to communicate—especially a command of such weight. Unbecoming in a supreme being, a god. God! If he wanted me to do it, he'd tell me in no uncertain terms. He'd erase any doubt.

But then it wouldn't be a test of faith. Would it?

Now the floor was buckling, giving.

God commands. I obey. Thy will be done or—

Or what? What have you got to lose? If it is God and you don't do it, eternal damnation. If it isn't God and you do do it— Well, if it isn't God and you intend to do it under the belief that it is His command, then surely he'll intercede and prevent you from doing it. Right?

Right.

The floor settled a moment.

But it isn't that straightforward. It's a test of faith, and I'm turning it into a test of fear. If I do it, I must be strong and sure. The minute I allow a flicker of doubt, of hate, of panic, or of hope for reprieve, then I will have failed, I will have been guilty of a terrible lack of faith. I must be willing, with my whole heart, to kill—

She cried out and the sound echoed up to the painted arched ceiling. It returned just as uttered.

… Thy will be done, Father said. Thy will—

But which will? 'Thou shalt not kill,' remember. His will is contradictory. It's irrational.

Ah—faith begins where thought leaves off. Remember Kierkegaard. It's precisely because it's unreasonable that you must believe. Do not cling to reason.

All right. Contradiction aside, it's still murder!

Yes, but again call on Kierkegaard—it is murder ethically. Ethics is social, relative, a duty to man. The issue here is duty to God. It is universal, absolute. You must suspend the ethical for that.

That's all very nice and maybe if it were my decision alone I could make that leap, but this concerns Peter and Joey. I can't prove my faith at their expense. That's selfish. It's unchristian.

Nonsense. It can't be unchristian to do God's will.

She was confused. Which supports were strong? And which wall did they support? How many walls were …

Thy will be done—

Thy will is—

Kathy groaned, sweat and tears running down her face. Then she slowly looked up again at the altar, to the crucifix hanging there.

Do I want to worship a God who would order such a thing?

She sank against the wooden back of the pew. She stayed a long while later, in prayer, battling again to keep the wall from crumbling completely.

It was dark by the time Kathy staggered up the steps to her door. Peter was waiting on the other side, worried.

"Kathy, where have—it's nine o'clock! The supper—Joey is in bed—" He stopped. "Honey, you shirt." He fingered it. "It's soaked." She looked up at him, puzzled.

"I was at the church."

He stared at her. Waited a moment. In vain. "That's all you're going to tell me?" His concern became indignation. She looked at him helplessly.

"No supper," she added and distractedly climbed the stairs to fall asleep on her bed.

September passed, witness to the increasing turmoil Kathy felt. It was like a tumor in her side. Her nerves became thin, and thinner when she realized she wasn't what she should be to a little boy starting school. She felt like an old woman, a very old woman. *I've so looked forward to all of this and now—* Peter watched questioningly, silently, then bitterly.

"Two more days until the weekend." Joey's chatter was more subdued than it used to be. He continued trying to cut up his meat. "Is this Thanksgiving weekend, Mummy?"

"Yes, it is, by gosh," Kathy exclaimed with an attempt at enthusiasm. Then feigning ignorance, she inquired, "What's that?"

"It's-a-time-when-we-all-give-thanks-for-what-we-have." Joey looked at his parents for approval. Kathy smiled, almost.

"How would you like to go on a hike this weekend—to see all the coloured trees and birds and chipmunks we have to give thanks for?"

"A hike? In the forest, you mean?" Joey's eyes grew wide. He looked at his father for final decision. He nodded.

"We can take some tuna and peanut butter sandwiches for a picnic, too!" she said with effort.

"Whippee!" Joey yelled. His glass of milk went over. He quickly looked down as the sober words came out. "I-spilled-my-milk-Mummy-I'm-sorry." There was barely a pause. "Can we really go?"

Joey clambered over a few more rocks then sat down at the top. Kathy was right behind him, puffing and sweating a bit.

"Oh, Joey, you go too fast," she said when she reached him and tousled the boy's hair. Joey stood up and declared, "It's a good thing daddy stayed down because this cliff is too high for him with all the sandwiches on his back."

Kathy laughed. "Yep, I think you're right."

Joey wandered toward the edge to look down at his father. "Don't go too close, Joey. Be careful." She heaved to her feet to stand beside him, but stopped. *As a test of faith, kill thy son.* The words hadn't let her go. She looked over at Joey. The words gripped her tightly. *As a test*—she started sweating anew and clenched her fists. *No fear, no doubt...I must— Thy will be done. Oh God I do love thee. I love Joey. I—* She bit her lip. The blood sealed her cries inside. Her knees trembled. *No hate. Our father who art in heaven...* She feverishly began reciting. *Thy will be done.* She turned in a circle, a caged animal. Joey bent down to look at a fern. *Hallowed be Thy name Thy kingdom come Thy will be—Joey! No hope for—*she gasped, grabbing for air, "Thy will be—" Joey turned, hearing his mother's raspy voice. "Mummy?" She started to lunge at Joey, blinded. "God Thy will be—" her screams overpowered Joey's. "Thy will be—" her body struck, her hand reached—he went over. "—done."

They walked past the rest of the cells. Another two were occupied by women lying on their cots; in the last, a figure was bent, on her knees, in the far and dark corner. They passed through the gates and stepped into the office.

"That last one. Was she praying?"

"Roberts? Yeah," he replied in a voice that discouraged further questions.

"Do many go religious after being committed?"

"No. Well. She's always been religious, that one."

The other man seemed surprised, but stubbornly persisted. "What's she in for then?"

The officer stopped his purposeless shuffling and looked into the other man's eyes. "Murder. Pushed her son over a cliff ten years ago. Pleaded guilty. Got sent here and been prayin' ever since."

The man's eyes shifted uncomfortably around the room. The officer continued to speak, to the air rather than to him. "Strange case, that one. Everyone wanted her to plead temporary insanity. She would've been better off for sure. But she insisted like a rock on a plea of guilty." He scratched his head out of habit. "If she wasn't insane then, she sure is now."

1976

I started to become an atheist (I was raised to be a Roman Catholic) in high school (thanks, KCI for offering a "World Religions" course!), and this story is one of my earliest expressions of doubt. See "The Great Jump-Off" in Particivision and other stories *for a later expression and* Thus Saith Eve *(a stand-alone ebook also in the collection* Satellites Out of Orbit*) for an even later and more comprehensive consideration (I even used "I am Eve" and "I am Mary, mother of God" for audio collages on my album,* The Art of Juxtaposition*). Lastly, see the earlier parts of* This is what happens. *(I have since moved from 'There is insufficient evidence for belief in god' to 'Religious belief is responsible for a great deal of unnecessary pain, not only physical—consider the Inquisition—but also psychological.')*

February 2021

Senior Citizens' Dance

and look at that one—
pink dress over the disintegrating figure
rhinestone necklace on the loose hanging neck;
I'll bet she was runner-up
to the queen of the prom;
the football player she loved is dead now;
so is the gas attendant
she married.

and that one—
the man with the pipe:
it went well with his bushy beard
as he graced the halls of the
university philosophy building;
now it's just another filthy habit
old men have.

another one—
he saunters
sort of
to the counter
and orders an orange juice;
a far cry from the

red caps of years ago;
he goes back carefully
to his wooden stack chair
successfully sits
and waits.

1977

let there be life—
then let there be death.
i want no streaks of gray
when my mind becomes confused
and my body, abused.
when the light is dying
let me put it out in rage

i shall never
life an unclenched fist of age.

1978

tears erode
    her earthen face
        waves   aging
  creases become crevasses.

        mist has long covered the peaks
   lying in relief
and she wandered along those disappearing summits
     lying in belief
till the lightening
left scars in her eyes.

the sediment of years collecting,
warm clay, stoning into hard.

1979

the wanting
  the wondering
    the waiting
for what?

1979

Two O'Clock Pick-Up

(from Memoirs of an Office Worker)

I wheel my cart around the office cabinets
and clumsily manoeuvre a stop at the first desk
to pick up the business miscellany
from her filing basket.

I feel like a beggar
poking around
separating the little yellow cards
and the green slips
from the letters.

Without raising her head to look at me
she casts another letter, a carbon copy
into her basket
for me to take and
blacken my fingers
—as befits a garbage collector.

1979

A Zoo

two very dead branches
crossed around a steel pole
held by a rusted wire—
oh yeah,
nature's artistic disorder

a half-dressed bird
perches foolishly—
below a branded sign
"The Great Horned Owl"

then to the bears—
at least there are two
misery loves a companion
and needs a comfort,
they lay close together
a discarded heap
on the concrete roller rink floor
that features three real rocks
cemented in place at the centre

this is a prison.

1980

and Pegasus
   hesitating
      looking back for me—
go, my silver stallion,

                        go on—

I cannot ride.

1980

Show and Tell

june 11 ... dear brad ... work on the *Pathètique* is going well. i have finished the first and second movements: the first is very exciting to play, one cant help but get caught up in the emotion of it—god i wish i could write like that; the second is just *so* beautiful—i cringe because i dont do it justice, i dont have the smoothness and the subtlety it deserves. tomorrow i shall begin the third movement.

would you believe i have found someone up here who has a grand? a yamaha no less. he is letting me play on it once a week, just for a few hours—not enough—not nearly enough! but still its better than nothing. certainly better than the second-hand upright i have. oh well. one makes choices. if i taught full time, in a few years i could have a yamaha grand too. but i'd have a lot less time for my work. no, i like it how i have it.

i finished a fugue yesterday! yes, i actually wrote a fugue—theyre much more fun to compose than to play. it turned out to be in the key of c minor. cant get away from that old diatonicism no matter how consciously i ignore the harmonies. i could go back and, say, naturalize all the b flats, so it'd be in a different mode, but what the hell, i wrote it this way because thats the sound i wanted.

now that it is getting warmer, Chestnut and i go for our walk in the evening instead of in the afternoon. the beach is quite nice at dusk. very peaceful. and Nut still runs ahead then comes bounding back then runs ahead again—such a joy to see him so free and happy. did i tell you he's become friends with Sheba? a german shepherd who's here at the same time. it is really quite amusing considering that Nut comes up to about

Sheba's knees, but they romp around quite delightfully. last time Nut didnt want to leave, and every ten yards or so he'd turn around, sit down, and look back toward the beach. all the way home.

i've started running again. its an anti-depressant and it gives me more energy to work—which is what i need now. i'm up to a nice five miles and wont go any further. i've given up the idea of a marathon, i shouldve done it three years ago when i was doing ten and fifteen mile distances. but now, well, i'm into other things, i guess.

love, amanda.

june 13... dear brad ... well i have finally finished my analysis of Gagnons music. you know his stuff is ridiculously simple and he uses repetition all the time. and its incredible how conventional his harmonic structure is. and yet, for all that, i find his music very beautiful, very satisfying. thats curious. perhaps i'm using my head too much when i compose, trying to avoid all the cliche patterns. but when i dont consciously attend to its composition, it turns out quite mundane, 'pretty' at best. maybe its just that Gagnon creates such touching, haunting, lyrical themes, perhaps their beauty carries the whole piece.

its been only ten days since you've been gone and already this is my fourth letter. i expect it'll slow down. sometime, soon, maybe.

yesterday i acquired two more new students. so that brings me back up to my minimum of twenty. no more worries about rent! and theyve both been taking lessons for a few years already—a nice relief among all the beginners i seem to have.

by the way, my idea of incorporating composition into the lessons by starting with sound effects seems to be going over quite well. most of the kids just love the idea of figuring out how an elephant falling down the stairs would sound or angels singing out of tune. a few days ago one came and did 'someone eating corn chips and chewing bubble gum at the same time'. neat, eh. after the sound effects, we move into telling a story while playing the soundtrack for it. i can hardly wait for that last kids stories!

Canary developed a painful rattle this morning. its at the garage now. hope its nothing too costly. maybe i shouldve kept your car after all, instead of selling it.

... love, amanda.

june 16 ... dear brad ... The National Academy of Music called today offering a job. if they had called a week or so ago i wouldve accepted, but i have enough students now, i dont need any more money. and anyway when you teach at an academy, they skim off half the students fee for themselves, so on my own i make much more per hour.

have finished analyzing Supertramp. i have always been impressed with their music—and now i've found that it actually *is* as interesting and innovative as it sounds. Hodgson sure likes to use the bVII chord.

work on my Pieces, Opus 2, continues to go slowly.

Anna dropped by the other day, 'to see how i was getting along'. she brought her photo album of her trip, apparently i need seme 'cheering up and distraction'. she says its unnatural to be alone so much, especially at a time like this. i tried to remind her that ive lived alone all my adult life and i like it that way, but, well you know Anna—

we actually spent a whole hour looking at those—those awful snapshots. they werent photographs, i cant call them that. i almost brought out all your work to show her the difference, but no, i didnt.

'thats us in those caves up at Collingwood, you know, where they make that blue mountain pottery ... and heres us at the Calgary stampede … here we are getting on the ferry to Vancouver Island … here we are getting off …'

my god. why do people keep photo albums. not for aesthetic pleasure, thats for sure. as a record of their experience, i suppose. no, its more than that, its a *validation* of their experience, their very existence. the album s something to show to other people: see, this is where have been, what i have done, here is proof, look, i exist.

funny how important, how necessary it is, to show and tell. how we need to verify our *subjective* existence by exposing it to an *objective* existence. a reality of the self depends on an interaction with a reality of the other.

and its the *giving* in that interaction that matters, not the *taking*—the transmission, not the reception. Anna didnt even notice if i was interested or not, if i nodded at the right time or asked a question here and there. it mattered to her only to be able to show the snapshots to me and tell me about them.

its like that old riddle, does a tree falling in the middle of the forest make a sound if no one hears—well, the tree doesnt care, that blessed oak or pine just needs to be able to fall. its existence is validated by the mere falling—whether it is heard or not is irrelevant.

                                        … love, amanda.

june 17 … dear brad … today when i looked at that picture of you i have one my billboard, you know, the one taken in your Vancouver apartment after we made love all morning—i suddenly realized that you are my snapshot, you are my way at validating my existence.

no, listen. when we talk about love, what do we mean? im not referring to that general love of humanity, that impersonal respect for individual life in all its manifestations—im talking about personal, specific, one to one love. what is it?

well, lets take away all the business that goes on between two people in a love relationship. take away the family business—the kids need new shoes, johnny went to the dentist. take away the household business— what do you think about new furniture for the den, dont forget to pick up the drycleaning. and take away the social business—the bowling league starts thursday. now what is left of this loving couple, what is left of their interaction, their relation? i had an awful day at the office, so and so called this morning, i did the basement rug: show and tell. thats what passes for love. just show and tell.

and we're no different. oh we dont have any family business—neither of us wanted to be the mother. we dont have any household business— we've lived apart, so each to their own, no need to interact on this dimension. and we dont have any social business—again, living apart leads to separate social circles, though neither of us is very social to begin with. yet we do have a relationship, we have had a very stable and satisfying love, for seven years.

this lack of 'business' in our relationship just makes it easier to see what that relationship, what that love is. and look—our telephone calls are like progress reports, our together times every two or three weeks are part piano recital, part photography exhibit: show and tell, affirming our subjective existences by showing and telling to an objective existence, the beloved. that is love. nothing else. nothing more.

… love, amanda.

june 18… dear brad … and in our relationship, in our love, its been the transmitting, not the receiving, that has mattered most—like the tree, it matters not whether i am heard. as long as i could say, hey listen, i finished that piece i was writing, or hey look, i tried this out and it worked. as long as i could talk to you, share my life with you, as long as i can show and tell to you, love you—then my life is valid, it is real.

so thats why im writing letters to you. weeks after your funeral.

… love, amanda.

1982

… and this is the behaviour modification class …

for children in need of verbal skill development …

i see the child
it is a herculean struggle for him
to form the sound "beh"
he is hitting his head with his hand again
and again and again
it has become a reflex action.
    which encrusted nerves are being twisted
    which cerebral fibres, singed
    as he chars a trail through brain tissue to connect,
    to connect …

two hours later he grunts "bah"
as if expelling a petrified stool.
a morsel of food is shoved into his mouth.

congratulations.

1982

Tears into the Sea

at the harbour dock
all fresh, all fascinates
the child peers down into the water
enraptured by the fish,
the fronds, the shells,
by the crab, most of all.
he watches, mouth open,
as it picks its way, strange way
to walk, how
can it walk like that,
he bends, watches closely, not close enough, so
curious, resourceful, with two sticks,
he lifts the crab up, out
to see this funny stranger.
it lands on its back on the hot concrete
helpless sickly white legs
grabbing at air, clutching,
he tries to turn it over
again, again
clumsy with the sticks
fearful of the claws, though
moving, waving slower now
not right, again, hurry
he tries again, cannot,
in panic, he shoves it over roughly

back into the water,
it falls onto the seabed
belly up
no longer struggling, no longer waving
still
lifeless.
and the cry, high pitched
wail of surprise, "It's dead!'
echoes across the waves
but I didn't mean to,
I didn't know, I
the child stammers
protesting ignorance, guilt, death
as tears fall into the sea.

1982

Recognition

silver on blue
they soar and sing
sliding on the whimsied wind
over the ocean.
every now and then
no—
every now
every moment they dive
less a ballet, more a jig
they screech in fierce play
carnival confetti
no—
they are fluttering hungry
to the flotsam:
a cobwebby mess of entrails.

catch carrion, survive.

grey on grey.

1982

Dissonance

"... under waterfalls or in mountain streams, you can have the bath of your dream, Booboo's Bubble Bath." The vocalist crooned into the mic, blond voice of a sensual child.

"Good—that's a take," Keith called out after he flipped the last switch on the control board. "Take a break and listen to the playback," he said from behind glass.

The musicians took off their headphones with assorted expressions of relief—this one jingle had taken two hours. Julie, on flute, sat down. Carol leaned her guitar against the stool and her self against the wall. Lex took her hands away from the keyboard and simply put them her lap. She stared at the keyboard. Two hours, one hundred and twenty minutes, on some stupid commercial for bubble bath.

"... from head to toes, aqua, lavender, pine, or rose, under waterfalls ..." What an imbecilic song. No, it wasn't even a song. Of course not.

"That was great, what you came up with on keyboards, Lex—super, just super. I like it," Keith said. "And Julie, the flute ..." Lex had opened the jingle with some arpeggios, cascading down the keyboard, at sixths. Of course it was good. It was very appropriate. It was very effective. It would sell. People would buy Booboo's Bubble Bath. The success did not please her.

She had promised herself she would stay with the studio only long enough to pick up some skills that her conservatory training had left wanting. She was not quick with transpositions, formula harmonies, or improvisation. But of late, each session of apprenticeship served not to enrich but to cheapen her self as a musician, as an artist.

"Jack'll pay you on your way out. Thanks, people." Thirty bucks apiece for a sixty second number, twenty for a thirty. Considering that it usually didn't take more than an hour, an hour and a half at most, to get one sixty down, the pay wasn't too bad. But then again, any pay wasn't too bad. Lex had decided a few years ago to forego the security of a regular job in order to have the time to compose. She got up to leave.

"Lexie, can you stay a bit longer?" He held up a reel, "The one we did last week, the burglar alarm? I was thinking about the intro you used—yeah, goodnight Carol—you know, heavy bass chords? Well, how do you think that thing of Beethoven, you know, 'da da da daaaaah'—how do you think that would sound instead?"

The silver pieces of Judas floated by. Glistening, transparent. If she touched them, they would burst into nothing. She knew that.

"Well, I don't think—"

"Aw sure, it'd be great! It would catch people, you know, because it's familiar—"

"But it's Beethoven's, isn't there a copyright or something?" she asked weakly.

"'Course not, it's in the public domain. Try it anyway, okay?" No, it wasn't silver. Some other colour held down the word 'no'.

She put her headphones back on and turned to the keyboard, hands waiting. He put the tape on, and she played it.

"Not sinister enough. Try it again. Put some feeling into it." She nodded to the voice in her ears. What kind of a feeling do you put into a betrayal? She played it again, fuller, doubling at the octave.

"Closer, but not quite. Maybe a bit slower, not so mechanically."

The warmth of the studio began to bother Lex and her hands began to sweat, a problem worsened by the plastic keys—ivory responded, absorbed; imitation could not. She played the motif again. This third time was sufficient to sever it from the ensuing symphony. The four notes lay powerless and pathetic at the ends of her bloodied fingers.

"There was a slight stumble on that one. Want to try it again or call it a night? There's no rush on this one."

She answered quickly, "Let's leave it."

"Okay. I'll hold onto it till Monday. Have a good weekend." She took off her headphones and set them on the keyboard. After gathering her stuff, silently, she picked up her thirty dollars and left.

She turned the key in the lock and entered her house. It was only nine-thirty, and she had intended to finish the first movement of a sonata she had been working on. The work had been slow. She wasn't yet fluent with the discords she was using.

She stopped in the kitchen to pour herself a drink. Then, as she turned on the light of her studio room, the portrait of Beethoven caught her conscience. She stared at it for a moment. Then she walked over and took the portrait off the wall. It didn't belong in this room anymore. A trade had been made. Suddenly she flung the picture onto the floor and—no, two trades. By using music not to move but to manipulate, she had forfeited her right to— She ripped the unfinished movement in two. Then left.

The bar was noisy and the dance floor was like a piece of still pulsing carrion, covered with crawling flies. It didn't matter maybe. She found a stool to sit on and ordered a drink. It took only five minutes for someone to ask her to dance.

"So do you come here often?" he asked as they traced the simple pattern.

"Only when I need a little extra cash."

There was a silence. But not a break in their rhythm.

"How much?"

"Thirty bucks."

There were no more words until the end of the number.

"Would you like to come back to my place for a drink?" he asked.

"Certainly."

Of course it's easiest to sell what you value the least. She had always been resentful of her body: it needed to be fed and watered, and had to have at least four hours of sleep in every twenty-four. Too, having been an athlete in university years, she knew its naked honesty, its pretensions to grandeur, its sad limitations. Unlike music, it had no lasting power or beauty.

So there was no violation in this. There was no sacrifice of integrity, no compromise of principle, no misuse of skill.

"Stay the night?" he asked afterwards.

"No, it's only eleven-thirty."

"Can I call you? Perhaps next Friday?"

"Sure. I'll leave my number."

Elated, she ran for a while. Some order had been restored; some hierarchy re-established.

Purged, she re-entered her house. Keith would still be up, mixing. "Hello?"

"Keith, this is Lex."

"Oh, hi—"

"Listen, I'm not available for any further recording sessions."

"Oh—"

"Goodnight." She hung up.

Released, she walked back to her studio and turned on the light. Beethoven was put back on the wall. Then she picked up the pieces of the first movement. She could finish it now. Now she could control the dissonance that had been threatening the unity.

1982

Although I had taken off my rose-coloured glasses with respect to seagulls, I apparently had not yet done so with respect to call-girls.

February 2021

aria for solo flute
blue and silver
        crystal mist morning
almond tea
flowering branch

1982

The English Teacher

How does it feel? To be on your own … I turn up Fieldstone, then onto East Street. *Like a complete unknown … like a rolling stone* … I pull into the high school's parking lot, and turn off the ignition. Dylan shuts up. So does his harmonica. (I once listened to that song for two hours straight, was I stoned. I musta been.) I sit in my car and prepare myself for the passing through. Each time I open the school doors and step onto the other side, a wave of culture shock hits me. I am a foreigner.

But pass through I will. I am The English Teacher. Shit, I'm on time for 'O Canada' again. First time I sat through it in a classroom, I was called down to the office. Naughty. "You aren't setting an example for the students." Damn right I'm not. I'll be no model of hypocrisy. 'The true north strong and free'? Come on. 'I'll stand on guard for thee'? I will not, I'm pacifist. 'With glowing hearts—' "You don't have to sing it, you just have to stand for it, it *is* our national anthem." Nationalism is an infantile disease, I footnoted Einstein. (It was Einstein who said that wasn't it?) I was dismissed. No detention.

And then 'The Lord's Prayer'. Oh god. I stand and look out the window at the garbage blowing in the wind. So they don't see the derision on my face. Quote for tomorrow's writing exercise: Religion is the opiate of the masses. (Marx?)

Then the announcements come on. I don't put in any announcements. I tried once, at the beginning of the year, but they censored it, can you believe it. It was to start a debating club, The Forum, and it read something like 'Does God exist? Should you burn your draft card? Is capitalism good? Is abortion murder? Should attendance be compulsory? If you're interested in issues like these, come out to Room 304 at 3:05 for the very first meeting of LCI's new club, The Forum.' They read, instead, 'A new club for debating will meet today after school in Room 304.' Too controversial, they said. What the fuck? What about the spirit of educ— freedom of— I don't understand.

Morning rituals over, it's time for class. I stare for a few moments at the rows of faces until a vague notion of habit moves me. I go towards the filing cabinet, but then stop. Suddenly conscious. I remember my self. The smartass sixteen-year-old in the fourth row sees my dawning incomprehension and says "What's wrong?" He'd love to see me stoned in class, but when I'm stoned, I call in healthy and don't come to class at all. (Actually that hasn't happened yet, but I can hardly wait, to hear the department head's response.) Shall I be honest and open with my students? Shall I say I don't know what the fuck I'm doing here? I tell him "Nothing" and open the drawer. The seizure has passed, Lethe rushes on.

I get the graded essays out of the cabinet. Ah yes, grading essays. Pick a number, any number, to represent the quality of this piece. I hand them back and allow a few minutes for insults and complaints. One guy comes up and says "Why did I only get a 64% and she got 66%?" Right. Account for that 2% difference on a ten-page essay read two nights ago after 25 and before 30 others. "You used a semi-colon incorrectly twice, and she used it incorrectly only once." He believed me. He went back to his desk. I laughed.

My god— I laughed.

I carry on with English class. Vivisection becomes dissection with the instruments of an *a posteriori* black bag. I mean what writer is conscious of the plot pattern of rising action, climax, and resolution, the four techniques of building suspense, and the three differences between direct and indirect characterization? Is that the essence of the study of literature? Class dismissed. No detentions.

What the fuck *am* I doing here? I who disdain and mock the public am now its servant. Ah and here comes one of the masters now. I'm not against parents. I even called each one, yes each one, in September to introduce myself and open the lines of communication. But when they come in and demand "Susie got 70s last year and she's failing your course this year why?"—I mean, what to say? Well she musta got really dumb over the summer? Or she had an asshole teacher last year who didn't know the difference between the Petrarchan sonnet and the Spenserian sonnet? (I don't know the difference either but.) Or having successfully maneuvered herself through puberty, she is no longer interested in dangling participles? Or well she's into drugs now, didn't you notice? I tell the mother I don't know and dismiss her. No detention.

Susie by the way isn't the only student who is failing. So are John, Shirley, Mick, Rob, Paul, Marie ... The failure rate of my classes last term was 45%. I got called down to the office for that too. Apparently it's supposed to be no higher than 20%. "Justify your figures," the man says. Well, I replied, twenty-nine of the thirty-six students who failed did not hand in at least ten of the twenty required assignments and tests. As well, all failing students were absent at least fifteen days during the term, that's three weeks of missed school. "Well we can't have a failure of 45%, that's too high." Oh. "Perhaps you could raise all the marks by 15%. Would that bring the rate down?" Well, yes. It would. "Fine then." (What language are you using?) It would also give six students a mark of 105% or better. "Oh no, that's too high. We can't have that. The computers can only handle two digits." Oh. (What language did you say you were using?) I was sent back to my room. Number 304.

I teach wearing my jeans, a shirt, and my hiking boots. (I could tell you what kind of socks too but it might not matter. I'm not sure anymore. What matters.) My attire seems to pose a problem. I was called down to the office, this was in September, and I was told that I'm to "Set an example by dressing properly." What's improper about my clothes, I asked. "Well maybe inappropriate is the ward." What's inappropriate about my clothes, I asked. They don't seem to hinder my ability to teach, I don't suddenly forget the material when I put on my jeans, my evaluation standards don't decline if I have jeans on— "Well there is an accepted convention regarding dress for teachers." Is an Accepted Convention kinda like a Commandment? Or are you saying its mandatory for staff to wear uniforms? If the latter, why?

A teacher in this department, they still talk about it, confessed to me the other day that he was very grateful for his suitcoat and tie during his first years of teaching because they gave him the authority and respect he needed to control the class. So that's why. I thought so. I told him every day you wear your suitcoat and tie, you're teaching the students that it's what's outside that counts and you thereby discourage them from looking beyond the facades, from reasoning; you perpetuate the mentality of evaluation on the basis of appearance, of 'You are what you look like', of 'Judge a book by—' It's funny, my dog acts on much the same basis: response patterned by sensory stimuli. He didn't understand me. The other teacher.

I mean I could wear a suitcoat and tie too, but then they'd all wonder if I really was a lesbian, and then I'd have to shave my legs pierce my ears pluck my brows curl my hair paint my face and varnish my nails to prove that I'm normal.

On hall duty. Someone has spray painted "John sucks Arnie" on the ceiling by the door to the outside smoking area. Every student coming in either tsks or laughs. I don't understand. When I read it, I just thought so what? I mean, who the hell cares?

After my last class, I got called down to the office again. They sure do show an interest in me. I told than that and added an apology for my inability to return the compliment. They almost dismissed me then, but remembered I was there to account for my truancy during the last two days of the exam schedule. I told him (him, they, synonyms here, see I am too learning) that I was not scheduled for any supervision on either day and as all my exams were graded, marks calculated, and the first month of third term prepped, I couldn't justify driving half an hour each way to spend six hours in the smoky staff room picking my nose. He couldn't justify it either, but I had violated the Board's rule and that was a no-no. Oh dear.

One last check in my mailbox before I leave for the day. Item. The written report of an evaluation by one of my superiors who sat in during one of my classes last week. Could I please sign each copy and return all but one. Observations: The class began at 10:31 a.m. A few students came in late, one as late as 10:37 a.m. Many of the students were sitting towards the rear of the classroom, fourteen of nineteen. Attendance was taken by the teacher. A definite homework assignment was not given. The class was generally well behaved.

Wow. What observation skills! The implications of this man's priorities, his understanding of what education is all about— Content is irrelevant, I see. We may have been discussing the function of the cilia in a two-toed paramecium on rainy days in February. However, what we *were* discussing was a story's theme: the desperate extents to which being an alien can drive one. The character in the story, able to understand and be understood by no one, starts talking to dandelions, and then kills himself.

1982

Hourglass

crystal eggs in golden frame
lie shattered by the relentless ocean,
disintegrating sandcastles
drift out
onto a bloodied beach.

1982

Double Soliloquy

We used to get along okay, you and I. It never used to be difficult, when I was your daughter. Oh I remember that—it was a long, a very long time. I was happy, innocent, fearing, unautonomous.   I was a lot like you.   Even carried a purse and put on make-up. For six days.

Dear Jasmine: I DID IT!! I lost ten pounds! I have been on a diet for 5 weeks, very skeptical, but I did it. I counted calories & increased my exercise & lost the sensible way. Only Dad and Cheryl know—I wanted to wait until I had it done to tell you …

Then something very encumbering broke. An amnion. And I started looking. No, seeing … and thinking … and feeling.   And then, (only then), was I my self.

It's not unusual to see me now, on the street—construction boots and denim, shades, helmet in hand. I teach three classes a day to pay the rent and spend the rest of my time, my life, at my will. I compose, I read, I write, I study. Far cries from the route, marked on the map you gave me, to a husband, two kids, and a house around the corner.

… So Jennifer Watson is married as you can see by the enclosed. Looks like it was a very low key wedding …

And far cries from you.

That's no accident—that's a choice i made.

… Let me know if you get an invitation to Scott's wedding …

OH HOW I HATE YOU! You, who are the measure of all things.

You who would crucify me with your eyes. Not for their power (alas, you have none), but for their pain. As I refuse to cross myself and murmur the compulsory chant at the dinner table.

You, so secure in your religion. Never asking a question unless you knew its answer. Roman Catholic you still insist. You have yet to explain how one can be born Catholic, born believing in some specific system— but you were. And you sit snug, smug, in stability, the measure of maturity, while I, still the struggling Adolescent, friend of Fyodor, run.

… Finally got a letter from Dave and Charlene. They're very religious now. (Did I tell you this?) I guess she has Dave converted. He does not drink anymore—no booze at all in the house. They are even tithing. And when I think of all the loans he's bad interest-free from us— You'd think if he had money to give away, he'd think of his parents first. The letter as a whole was rather sickening. I was thanked for bringing up such a fine son, and it was signed "love in the Lord". Oh well …

I remember a comment you once made. It was after I moved out in my fourth year, then went out west for a while, rented a piano, lay on Wreck Beach, put in part-time at Office Overload, took an art course, had a bike accident, wrote a play, hiked in the mountains, before coming back with Pete and getting my B.Ed. at Queens. I remember you said, happily and with relief, "Well, we're glad to see you're getting back on the right track."   Oh god.

You know, Icarus and his father—they're nothing compared to you and me.

… We sold your/our piano—rather sad—seems like a little more of you leaving us. It goes tomorrow. I still have some of your paintings on the walls downstairs which remind me of you though …

I remember a few comments you failed to make, too. Like when I eventually had some poetry published, you did not ask to read the work. Oh no, you were much more interested in how much the magazine paid. And like when for years I was downstairs at the keyboard practising, composing, you did not ask to hear my latest piece. You shut the door so the sound wouldn't carry up to the kitchen.

By the way, this is one of the poems:

like a bird in a cage
—bars of love—
i am hung
in this household.

i cannot sing soundlessly
—muted strains—
yet every note aloud
hurts.
unheard.

i wonder
is a sound a sound—
am i if—

i must—
i can—
i am to fly!
and i will beat my strength against these bars
till i am free.

(and someone will whisper
there has been a bird in the house.)

It is titled "to mom and dad".

... Glad to hear you are using the blender—how does it mix powdered milk?...

Let me tell you something else I remember. A skirmish in the field of my pending teacherhood. The topic at large was respect and its relation to my attire in the classroom. You were saying that students don't respect teachers who are their friends. I asked you to name three people you respected—you could name only one but I passed over that—and the person you named was your former boss. When I asked if you didn't respect any of your friends, you shrugged and easily admitted what I'd seen a long time ago and wondered at. You said, "I don't have any friends." You know, it never bothered you. Why? Because you've always thought that that was the fault of the people you had met or had not met. (Oh, I hear you say, 'I *admit* I have faults!' Yes, but you can't forgive yourself for having them, candidate for sainthood as you're striving to be; you admit your humanness without genuinely accepting it.) You've not once thought that your friendlessness was a reflection of you. You who are so impenetrable, you who are so safe in your sheltered niche. You have not yet realized the vulnerability of naiveté, the reason your defenses are so thick that even I cannot touch you.

… I should tell you I suppose, that I am not writing to Dave & Charlene anymore. When I get a letter from them, they make me physically & emotionally upset & I would rather not have that. References to me in the letters seem hostile & I do not know why I am being treated this way. What have I done to deserve this? Of course I am sick about it, but that is the way it is. Dave didn't even remember his Dad on Father's Day, not so much as a card or a short note, and I think that is just terrible …

I tried once. That one night soon after I got back from Vancouver. I had stopped on the way in Edmonton to talk to Dave. Noble me, I was going to play mediator on a king's horse and put my mother and her son back together again. Well needless to say, it did not work. Oh it went well with Dave: he listened to your side as I interpreted it, realised a few of his bad moves, explained his side to me, and discussed avenues of amends. But you: I couldn't present three words of Dave's side before you raised your shield, dropped your visor, and readied your lance.

I couldn't reach you in love. How can someone else, in friendship? You won't let anyone come near you. Not even yourself.

... oh by the way I have finished the crewel embroidery for Cheryl, so let me know about one for you—maybe I won't start until next Fall though, so you have time to pick one out ...

Funnier thing about that night though: I was moved to tears when I saw the vast extent of your insecurity, and I cried for you; but you cried for you too— (one of the few times I actually saw you cry, I might add): your capacity for self-pity surprised me. I realized wryly, 'like mother, like daughter' (I have examined the nature of my depressions).   You're better at it though. Much better.

... I do understand your depression. I too have had a good many times of downers. Kept it to myself I guess & also got myself out & up again. Mothers must or should be strong for their children & we tend to set aside our feelings, putting others first—over the years, this becomes a habit & so we go through life keeping our moods—if possible—& thoughts/hurts to ourselves ...

Your capacity for martyrdom has also surprised me. You would be a smiling Sisyphus, a silent Prometheus. Someone tells you 'you should do this, you must do that,' and you do! Without question, without comment. When will you realize that the someone is you. Only you.

I recall being so hopelessly tangled in a cobweb of shoulds (self-spun, of course, though at your direction) that I lost touch of my wants. There was no space for the real in my superstructure of holy ideals. And I had been taking it for granted that I should live according to those *shoulds*. Beyond the satisfaction of fulfilling a duty, I felt no happiness. And no wonder—I was denying so much of myself, not expressing, not exploring. You follow your inflexible code, of ethics, I suppose, at the expense of yourself! Well I will not perform such self-sacrifice. Not any longer.

I have realized that I have a choice. Actually, that I have been choosing all along, primitively, unconsciously. I used to think that it took more strength, more courage to walk the straight and narrow path, strewn with thorns, but conscious choice amidst the wide and meandering stairway is much more difficult.

… We see more than you think—don't forget we have been living on this earth for over fifty years—& I know you better than you think I do. You are, after all, my daughter …

You see, quality of life is not attained by an adherence to an inherited all-purpose prescription followed without exception; nor by experiencing everything to its fullest, as I once believed, during a spell of desperation— that is merely quantity of life. No, quality of life is attained by choice, by an intentional, discriminate selection of experience. Which can only be done by the individual for the individual. So I must not fold, bend, or mutilate my self. I must let it be, and study it. This is a difficult and complex task (which is why I laugh when you so lightly remind me that you know me well: I don't; you can't possibly. But it is a task which is prerequisite, essential. When I understand what I am, I can then begin to understand what life is. One cannot hope to understand what a tree is simply by standing, waiting, beside it for fifty years. (Portrait of my parents, as Estragon and Vladimir …)

… Last week we had bad weather for a couple of days & had water in the basement again. No damage, thank goodness, and it can be fixed in spring …

I know that my decision not to come home for Christmas hurts you. I know it hurts a lot. But the truth is, I don't enjoy your company. In fact, I can't stand it.

Remember just a while ago, I stayed there, at 'home', for two weeks while on a teaching placement. I found it very difficult, very exhausting. Living with you is like walking on a sheet of stretched plastic wrap: I have to tread lightly, very lightly, just upon the surface; the minute I abandon the small talk, the minute I ask about an opinion, an attitude, or truly answer your mock-sincere 'How are you?' or 'What's on your mind?'—it snaps. Tears apart. The edges curling into themselves …

… Are you eating much? …

And what's worse is that you continue to see yourself as bestower of advice, figure of authority, minister of approval: if you can't relinquish the role of parent, go find someone else to play child. (Can you define your self in no other way but in relation to me? That is, as 'mother'? I will not bear the burden of your identity-dependency hang-ups ...)

No, I'm spending my time with Pete, where openness is a risk worth taking.

... You said you were spending Christmas with Pete instead of with us. And I said I thought he'd be spending it with his family. Most children do spend Christmas with their families, you know. However, you were right when you said I had just assumed that. But so I assumed ...

Oh yes, you invited Pete to cone too. Funny, that was only after I had said no. The first two times you had asked, his name wasn't even mentioned.

But, I know. I know how you feel about us. You don't recognize our relationship. We aren't married and for some reason you think two people must have a priest's blessing and/or a judge's permission before they can love each other. And certainly before they express that love physically.

... perhaps your father and I could come visit you some weekend ...

You know what would really be funny? If for some bizarre reason you and dad came for overnight, and I told you that you had to sleep in separate rooms, because I choose not to recognize your relationship (it is not signified in terms I approve of) and that since this is my house, you must abide by my rules. That would be priceless. I'd love to see your reaction. Perhaps it would resemble my reaction when you did that to us. Think so?

... Not much else to say—still sewing and babysitting—I am taking the 18th off and Dad, Cheryl, Billy, and I are going shopping at Square One. Cheryl and I went shopping yesterday downtown & guess what—Dad babysat—even changed Billy & gave him a bottle. Now he says 'no sweat', 'anytime'... He was a little uneasy about it because it has been a long time since he had to do it for you, but some things you never forget ...

I remember you wouldn't talk with me about sex when I was thirteen (I recall a hand-me-down, *You're a Woman Now*, written by some nun), yet when I was twenty-one, you had the nerve to call me a slut. Do you remember the first time you called me a slut? I'm sure you do. It was around the time of Dave's wedding maybe two years ago. He had brought along his roommate, Jack, from Alberta for a holiday. Well Jack and I, among other things, took off to Toronto for a few days. You were horrified when you found out. And you asked—I think this was the third in a series of interrogatives—"Did you stay in a hotel?" I said "yes" and at that point reminded you that some things are private, but went on to explain, however, that I would not lie to you. Heedless of my words, you continued, thinking, I suppose, that all of this was your business. "Was it a two-bedroom suite?" I said "no". You seemed so unable to understand, and if I remember correctly, you even had to ask if we slept in the same bed then or did he sleep on the floor. You were shattered, and called me a slut. I wanted to— I said "Mom, look at me." But you said, with utter disgust, "I can't." "I want to talk about it." You would not. You could not face that truth. How many others have you refused to see?

… perhaps you can come home for Easter …

Do you remember the second time? That was just a few weeks ago. You didn't actually resort to labelling this time, but made a very heavy inference from scanty evidence which you didn't even care to confirm. I told you that I would appreciate it if you didn't leap to judgments about my character based on your assumptions about my sexual behaviour. I again invited you to discuss it. Again you refused.

… I bought Bill an outfit to wear to watch Cheryl and Art play baseball at the club. Next week is their first game. The outfit is red & white striped overalls with an applique on the bib which says 'Play Ball'—hat to match—a white with red & blue trim T-shirt which has a baseball & bat on the front. Then of course he had to have red canvas shoes to finish it off. They haven't seen it yet—I intend to have Billy model it on Sunday. Neat eh?…

So fine. Now I refuse. I've tried for seven years to persuade you to talk with me. But I have met resistance time and time again. You've too much to lose: your pride, your precarious equilibrium, your insecurity defenses.   Your reality. So, I'm through.

To forgive and forget would be to deny reality.

But do not think me thankless in my rejection. I recognize and am grateful for what you did and/or intended to do for the first fifteen years of my life. But a love of gratitude can only go so far, and I have gone as far as I can go.

The rest of our relationship lies only on a shared past. A past which is now dead.

… the enclosed treats were in the freezer—should be okay. Take care, love as always, Mom.

By the way, this dramatic monologue, this soliloquy, is just that, and not a dialogue, partly because you always complained about ending up so defeated whenever you argued with me, so why should you bother, you said. Well, yes, that is probably so. You usually do get backed into a corner when you argue with me. But this is why.

Dave has something to show for his business degree—he knows all sorts of things, marketing procedures, time study analysis, statistics, accounting, contracts, management —he has a job in an insurance company.

You thought I was throwing my intelligence away on a useless degree in philosophy and literature. Why are you so blind to what I have gained from my years at university, in class and out? Let me tell you, I've thought a lot, about a lot of things. And I'm a damned good thinker too. I'm trained to be clear, and thorough, to say well what I want to say about my ideas and feelings. And I'm familiar with positions and counterpositions, attitudes, and opinions, and perspectives, on all sorts of things—like truth, beauty, reality, right and wrong, life, death, and love—

But you're right. It is useless.

1982

Double Exposure

She turns off the busy street onto a residential avenue. A sudden still life. Solid brick houses, paved driveways, grass recently cut, flower beds doing respectably well. She knows what each living room looks like. Certainly one had a living room. And two tvs, curtains on all the windows, and a good set of china for guests.

She is a guest now to the driveway she pulls into. It used to be her driveway. She used to park her bike, the old 350, inside the garage. Before that she parked her bicycle there, behind her sister's behind her brother's. Now the driveway is her parents' driveway. And she is just visiting—no hardly that—not that at all really—she stays only a minute. Just long enough to drop off Chestnut for dogsitting. Certainly not long enough to use the good china.

Goodbye to all that. She had said it three or four years ago. Moved out of the snapshot setting in her fourth year, (too late, far too late), finished her first degree, went out to Vancouver, came east again to Kingston after a year or so, got a teaching degree, then went up near Barrie to accept a position, part-time so she could continue composing. With that last move, she rented a farmhouse and it seemed only natural that she finally have custody of Chestnut, who was by this time a burden to her sister with a baby and a two year old, and a threat to her mother because of all the dog hair and what if he ever piddled on her wall to wall carpeting.

She hates the arrangement. But Pete lives in an apartment, with two cats, and she could never leave Nut at a kennel. This way it involves only an hour of extra driving. But it involves seeing her mother once a month.

She moves away from the kitchen window as soon as she sees the blue car turn the corner, and prepares to meet her daughter at the door. It is hard, very hard, to see her only once a month, for all of forty-eight seconds at a time. But a year or so ago, she had received the letter declaring that their relationship was over, and saying, virtually, that she wanted nothing more to do with her parents. She would've liked to protest, but the letter seemed to forbid any response. It was put away in the cedar chest. She would respect her daughter's wishes, however little she understood. For almost two years now, the painful wondering why intensified every time Chestnut was to be delivered. Monthly depression had recurred, just transferred from one source to another.

It is difficult, getting more difficult, not to burst out and cry once, *Why?* But no. It is not her place. Not her right. When someone closes a door to you, you cannot just walk through, unannounced, uninvited. Even to knock would be rude, pushy. No. She must be patient, and wait. And hope that one day it will open again.

This is the tricky part. Still. She wouldn't feel right ringing the doorbell of her own home, what had been her own home; and surely that would hurt her mother even more—a final stamp of formality confirming their distance. But, in view of the distance, the logically consequent divorce she had enacted, nor can she just walk in. They were strangers, after all. Fortunately her mother meets her at the door. Again.

'Hi.'

'Hi.'

'Well. Here's Chestnut—Nut!' She calls to him; he is making the rounds, sniffing all the trees.

'How has he been?'

'Okay. Still perky as ever. That swelling hasn't come back. Must've just been bumped or something.'

'Well, that's good.'

'So. I'll be by to pick him up sometime on Monday.'

'Okay. I'll have him ready.'

'Okay.' She turns to leave.

'Wait— Stay—' She adds what must be the explanation for this deviation—'I want to talk.'

The daughter stops in surprise and confusion. Well. You want to talk. It's taken you two years. Finally it all matters to you, does it? Finally you care enough to want to talk about it? Well, now it's my turn. For all the years while I was living here, every time *I* wanted to explain, to ask, to work through, you walked away, you had something better to do. I swore I'd do the same if ever you decided *you* wanted to talk.

'Please—' She reaches out her hand in an uncharacteristic gesture.

The shutter is still stuck. Please. Then one such gesture seems to call for another. The daughter steps through the door, calling to Nut.

The mother, too, is surprised and confused. She had not intended to do this. If Cheryl or Dick were here, they would all sit in the family room, watch tv, and talk about something or other while she made the dinner. But it is not dinner time and they are not here. She can't just sit down and talk—that is frivolous, there is work to do. The house was silent and empty, except for the dishes clattering as she put them in the sink.

'Well?' Her daughter's voice demands. It always did. Her own daughter intimidated her. How foolish, she thinks, I am twice her age.

Pressured to say something, she asks, 'How's Pete?'

Then she realizes it is none of her business, each person's love is private, I should not have pried. She vigorously wipes off the counter, as if to erase the question.

Well, another first. I've been with Pete for five years now and I believe this is the first time you've ever asked about him. But of course, we're not married.

'Oh we're still happy as ever in our illegitimate relationship'—why should she be kind—'still fornicating from time to time.'

The mother turns sharply from where she was fussing. Then quickly turns back. A long pause follows. Not even the dishes dare disturb the concentrated emotion.

Then slowly her voice breaks through, pleads, 'What have I done to deserve all this?'

So here it is. Finally. She knew it.

'Deserve all what?' she sighs. 'This is not a punishment. I just don't like you anymore. What does anyone do to deserve not being liked? People just change, that's all. We're just very very different now. Surely you can see that.' She thought her letter explained all this.

'But you never see us anymore, you never—'

'Do you associate with people you don't like? Look, I could visit. We could get together and talk about the weather. Or we could talk about your sewing, your new furniture, I could 'tolerate' or 'humour' you, like friends suggest. But that's condescension, and a worse insult than pretense, to what we are. Why can't we just let it end?'

'But I'm your mother!' Doesn't that mean anything anymore, she wonders.

'So what?' Her voice raises and becomes louder. Nut slinks out of the room. 'Do you want a friendship out of obligation, out of gratitude? You're my mother. What difference does that make, now. I mean what does that mean?' She glares at her mother, who still believes in The Family.

'Yes. You need to ask. You wouldn't know,' the mother answers quietly. As soon as she says it, she regrets it. The disappointment, the resentment was not true anymore. This one was not Cheryl, this one was a composer and a poet, not a mother. She was right to leave mothering to those who had nothing else. Like herself.

The daughter freezes. She could've hit her mother then. Would've if she had been near enough. But she isn't. Is never near enough to her mother.

'That still bothers you doesn't it? Here I am twenty-five and I have no children. So I must not be grown up yet, I must not be a woman yet.' Her words froth on, 'Well let me tell you I'm more of a woman than you, because I'm a person! Mine is a conscious deliberate existence, not some boring series of conditioned responses. And a woman is a person first, wake up, the law was changed years ago, we are not just penis receptacles and reproductive machines. That's what *you* wouldn't know,' she adds quietly.

The last comment is a blow that knocks the air out of her. She was going to say, no, I used to think every woman had to have children before she lived her own life but I've changed my mind, I know now that not all women are meant to be mothers, just as not all men are meant to be fathers— But she couldn't say it now. She couldn't say anything for a moment.

The daughter quickly considers that her last accusation probably wasn't all that accurate. She doesn't think her parents had sex very often, and they did have only three children. But her mother has always felt the sex and the childbearing to be duties, that was what she meant to say.

The mother continues washing a few dishes. The daughter picks up Nut, who has crept back into the room. The house is silent and empty again. But the shapes and colours are a little distorted now. A Sabattier effect.

'I care about you,' the mother tries again. To explain.

'Why?'

'Because you're my daughter.'

'So?' Her voice is tired. Of trying to explain.

'So I've always cared about you, it's difficult to stop.'

'I should think I'm making it easier for you,' she smiles wryly.

'No,' the mother is very definite. 'No matter how insolent and belligerent you become, I will still care for you. That is love.'

The daughter feels humiliated and quickly counters. 'Well you have had a weird way of showing it. How often did you listen to my compositions? How much of my poetry did you read? You never wanted to hear the kind of music I played, and my poetry didn't rhyme, you complained.'

'Oh, be a little fair! If we showed interest, you accused us of being insincere because we really didn't like Bach or whatever, and if we didn't show interest, you accused us of not caring. How could we win?'

She never saw it that way before. And now that she does, she can't deny it.

'I loved you the best I knew how,' the mother continued, 'but that wasn't enough. You wanted love on your terms.'

Did she? She has to answer yes. Then she looks up, and returns the charge, neutrally, 'Don't we all?'

The mother's hands pause, holding the tea towel. 'We're only human,' she says, accepting her daughter's observation.

But the comment is misunderstood, 'Then why did you play god for your children! Never let them see you weak, uncertain, or selfish! No, always the dependable, responsible, unwavering tower of strength and virtue. Is it any wonder they turn against you when they discover it's a front?'

There is another pause. Time is needed to follow the sudden shift in foreground. She manages to focus on it. 'Yes, you once said that I was a bad mother.'

The daughter is struck by that. How can I say that of anyone? I who would be no mother at all should be the last to criticize any who accept that self sacrificing, that Christ role.

Then she remembers. 'I was fifteen when I said that, and it was a conditional statement. I had said that *if* you had us, expecting, wanting only replicas of yourself and not individuals, *then* you were a bad mother. Don't you agree, mothering should not be an ego thing—'

Of course she agrees. But then why is she having so much trouble giving up her daughter? Maybe she is, after all, the kind she reads about, the mothers who can't let go. The hands drying the dishes suddenly slow. No, this is not a matter of letting go. This is a matter of being let go, being rejected, by my own daughter.

The conversation is not over. The daughter wonders at the lull. She puts Nut down, opens her mouth as if to speak to her mother's back, then picks him up again. She wants to offer to help with the dishes. But the activity is just an escape from face to face confrontation, and she would not assist in that.

'Why don't you leave the dishes?'

'For who?' she snaps. 'Think your father is going to do them without me having to ask?' That is true. She saddens at her mother's reality. And then realizes that she herself can see further and reach higher only because she stands on the bruised and bloodied shoulders of women before her, women like her mother. Then why does she keep pulling me down, demanding I be the same, like those before me, like her?

She picks up another plate. Pete probably does. Without being asked. She envies her daughter, success in so many areas of her life. 'I often said that of the three of you, you were the one I'd worry least about,' she continues aloud.

The daughter is surprised, then pleased. Then angry at all the loss. 'Why didn't you ever say it to me? It might've helped to have known.'

She hadn't thought why before. 'Oh I guess it's the squeaky wheel that gets all the grease. The other two seemed to need more attention, more encouragement just to get by. You, you were always able on your own—'

'But then—'

'You'd think,' she doesn't let her interrupt, doesn't accept the blame this time, 'that in all your great perceptive insight, you would've recognized that as a compliment. But no, you only hear a compliment in the form you want, or maybe it didn't suit your purposes to hear one from me.'

Why would she say that? It's so completely wrong. I've always wanted to hear a compliment from you. Wanted so badly. 'Or it never suited your purposes to give me one,' she retaliates. 'Whenever I did something good, it was because of you or just luck or something. Like those straight A report cards, taken for granted because I was just naturally smart, not because I studied hard. Only the things I did that seemed bad were due to me. Remember I used to write out my own birthday cards to you, making up my own little poems? You thought it was in bad taste not to buy a card, so you decided I made up my own because I was lazy or because I forgot to buy one. It couldn't have been because I wanted it to be original, my own personal thing from me to you.'

The mother's face sags. Is that true? Did she really say that? But she kept some of those cards. They are still in the cedar chest.

'You never looked beyond your own interpretation of my behaviour,' the daughter continues with vengeance, 'just like when you called me a slut.' There. It was the wrong shutter speed and the wrong F stop but it was done. The scene was recorded now, committed to objective reality.

The mother puts down the tea towel. Lets it fall. So here it is. Finally. She opens and then closes her mouth, like an old woman with no teeth. There is a silence.

'I can forgive the name calling,' the daughter continues. 'It is difficult not to be a product of your time. But what hurt more than that was not being valued enough to talk about it. Not being given the chance to explain, to justify. It seems I was never worth discussion. Only humoured for my strange ideas and warned that my intelligence or my sensitivity was showing. Dave was listened to. Cheryl never had anything to say. Neither did you.'

The mother takes a few steps and sits in a chair at the small table. You too, you never looked beyond your own interpretation, she wants to say. 'I'm sorry', she says. Instead.

'Well. It's taken you three years.'

'Oh I must've said I was sorry at the time.'

'No. You didn't.'

'How can you remember for sure?'

'I don't remember.' She pauses. 'I wrote it all down. I wrote everything that was said. In my journal. It was the only way I knew to purge myself of the pain.'

Now I write everything I wanted to have said.

1982

the quill pricks
and i spill my passion
upon sheets of parchment
the wasted drops
dry before they moisten
leaving stained symbols
like scars

1982

The Egg Lady

"The piano teacher is here."

Mommy, the egg lady is here. She no longer lives on a farm. She is not married now. And that was fifty years ago though she is only twenty-five. But the rest is the same.

It's the rich houses that bother her most. She comes around to the back door by the swimming pool which is covered now, knocks twice, then enters. There is no need to stand on formality, they are expecting her. But even the Fuller brush man gets to use the front door.

"Wanna see my new skis?"

"Sure." She prefers their relationship to be friendly rather than fearful, but she is not here to look at skis, she is here to teach music.

After the appropriate oohs and ahs and questions to convince him of her interest, they sit down at the piano and begin the lesson.

"Okay, let's warm up the fingers—Hanons number one, right hand, legato."

He begins to play. Like a mechanical toy.

"Keep it smooth, that's—" One routine response attracts another, but she catches herself and does not put her voice on automatic pilot this time. It takes an effort. "Think of peanut butter," she says.

"Okay, now the left hand, staccato this time."

He jerks along, intent only on getting from C to C and back again.

"Slow it down, control it ..." He doesn't hear.

The mother walks in softly and sets the little tray on the table beside her chair. A large glass of milk and a plate of cookies. Sometimes it made her feel like a child (would the woman offer milk and cookies to

Bartok?), but she was grateful—tea was cheap and she drank a lot of that, it was milk that seldom went on sale. Besides, the gesture was very generous. She mouths a thank you and turns back to the boy.

"Okay, scales in C: whole tone, chromatic, major, then minor." She tries to stay spirited, to encourage life into his fingers. But she knows how ridiculous an enthusiastic egg lady looks. He dutifully goes through the motions. Of all four scales.

"Now, The Bird Song, you were to transpose it from C major to G major." He does so.

"And now, what mode did you make up for it?"

"C with F sharp and A sharp."

"Okay, let's hear it."

This is supposed to be an exciting part of the lesson. Discovering weird sounds, exploring … He doesn't seem excited. She herself hadn't even heard of modes until she was in grade 8 or 10, and it was still very difficult for her to play, listen to, or compose anything that was not diatonic. Don't you understand, she wanted to shout, I am consciously and carefully exposing your virgin ears to a much wider spectrum of colours, *you* won't be entrenched in the mire of major-minor modality, don't you see, I'm setting you free, I'm—of course not. I'm only the egg lady. He forgets to sharpen all the Fs except one.

"How did you like that sound?"

"It was okay." Nonchalant.

"Composition next. You were to pick a feeling and play how you think it would sound on the piano," she says eagerly. They'd started with simple sound effects, then moved into emotions, then story lines, then free comp. How lucky these children were. To start so young. To be encouraged to create, to express themselves—

"Uh … I didn't get that part done."

"Oh." It wasn't the first time he hadn't completed all of his assignments. "Did you have trouble? Which feeling did you pick?"

"I couldn't decide." Had he tried?

"Oh." Maybe he needed more direction. "Well let's say you try anger for next week." Frustration would have been too subtle.

No response.

"Would you rather leave out this part of the lesson for a while?"

"Yeah."

"Okay." You cannot force.

"Mozart, the minuet?" He turns to page twenty-one in his conservatory book. And hacks his way through. Would he have the nerve to do this if I were Rubinstein?

"How often did you practise this piece?"

"Maybe two or three times."

"Each day?"

"No. All week."

"Uh-huh. And why is that?" She knows, in the competition between Mozart and Atari, Mozart had lost again.

"I didn't have time."

"Well, you have as many hours in a day as everyone else. It's how you use them that counts. You probably won't be able to play well if you don't practise, you know that." Of course he knows that.

They finish with a bit of ear training and sight reading. She had hoped for a few minutes between lessons (both of the children had lessons, of course) to play her latest composition on their piano. A Yamaha grand. It would feel so beautiful, she knew it— But the girl is standing by, ready.

"Hi," she says brightly, putting aside her disappointment.

"Hi."

The lesson is much the same. Too much the same. It's difficult for her to keep enthused, to pass on to them her passion for music, when she is, after all, just the egg lady. Intent is always limited, no, dictated by expectation. She used to criticize those, especially women, who would complain of others, especially men, that they weren't letting them do such and such or be so and so. She used to think that that attitude, that needing permission or consent, revealed an acceptance of inferiority and passivity, but she knows now that it reveals an acceptance of something far different: an acceptance that all existence requires co-operation, all identity is an agreement.

In half an hour, the mother reappears, purse in hand.

"I'll have to cancel next week's lessons," she says, picking out the correct change. "We're taking the children to Quebec."

It only takes three or four cancelled lessons to put her rent payment in jeopardy. "Would you like a make-up lesson before you go?" she asks politely. "I could come Monday," she bends over backwards.

"Oh, no, they'll be too excited," the woman laughs as she hands her the money.

The week after next was school holidays. It would be a lean month. "Okay," she laughs too, understanding. The shortage of money bothers her far less than the attitude that she can be dismissed so capriciously, that there is no responsibility to have a make-up lesson or pay for missed lessons, that she is not worthy of a contractual agreement.

She cannot afford to tell her to go to hell. "Well, have a good holiday," she says.

"Thank you, see you in three weeks then."

"Yes." The laundry lady will come on Tuesday, the cleaning lady, Wednesday, and the egg lady, Thursday.

1983

Demonstration: July, 1983

marching in a mirage
of island existence
oblivious to the lines that connect

                    connect

they shout cry and whisper
seeking the sound of freedom
the sound of one hand clapping.

                                        1983

The Pietà

He receives her in silence. As if his interacting with anyone were a sacred event.

The solemnity bothers her, it makes her uneasy. Not, she thinks, because she is self-conscious, but rather because she is too aware of the ridiculousness of his gravity. It is ridiculous because she is the object of worship in this back room behind the laundromat—but this she does not realize. She is a woman, though, and should be used to it. But then no, it has only been since she turned twenty-two or -three that she has been seen as woman—so she has had little experience with this pattern of response. (And he so clearly sees her as woman. Is it because he is so uncertainly man? Do homosexual men—well, bisexual men—define women with sharper lines in order to appear clear about their own sexual identity? She didn't know.) At least he has stopped calling her Patty. She will wait for the third name.

Though the absence of small talk is pleasing, she attempts to compensate or cancel or ignore the hallowed hush. She finds the image of monk under vow of muteness welcoming her into his cell as if unfolding a beautiful flower, a little pretentious. He has no cowl.

"I had to come to town to deliver a score, so I thought I'd drop by." Funny she should call Toronto a town. She herself lives on Lake Simcoe, part of (well not really) a small community that didn't even have a population sign.

"So this is your new place," she says, hating to resort so soon to the social convention. But she knew he wouldn't accept it, there is no danger of a guided tour requiring correct hums and hahs.

"Yes," he answers definitely, and with an unexpected pride. His movements are slow and wondrous as he finds a place for her jacket.

He had moved two or three months ago. She had called once in the summer and asked to see his work. He had been surprised. An indication of how misunderstood everything still was, since she had thought the event was long overdue and had wondered why it was by request and not by invitation. (But then, she was still waiting for him to ask to hear some of her work.) About a month after she had visited him to see a few paintings, he had called. This had surprised her. Up until then—that is, since their initial meeting and parting three years ago—all the attempts to 're-kin' had been initiated by her. It was she who had written several times, it was she who had appeared at his doorstep. She had decided that this lopsidedness was responsible for some insecurity on her part. Am I pushing myself onto him, does he want to see me, does he think wont this bitch ever let go? And that insecurity, that uncertainty about his evaluation of her, made her overly defensive. It was this defensiveness that had left their first attempt in ruins: after five intense and exhausting hours, they both simply gave up and left the field. The second attempt, a year after that, when she had come to see his work, was also almost lost several times; but they managed, just, to keep balanced on the fine line between worthwhile upset and futile outrage. This visit is her third, but at least his phone call has intervened. He said he would like to visit her sometime, but he had just moved and was working on renovations, a lot had to be done, but the place was ideal, he planned to stay for a while this time, he had arranged to tend the adjoining laundromat, full-time now, maybe only twenty hours a week later, so he couldn't come up yet, the laundromat also needed a lot of cleaning and fixing up.

"Yes," he repeats eventually, and lifts his hands. "I raised the ceiling a bit and put in those windows. It was far too dark. I needed the sunlight," he says, his voice heavy with conviction. It sounds like a rationalization.

"And I have learned so much," he continues. "People think they need to apprentice for years before being able to do work like this. It is an illness of our society, this horrid underestimation of human potential and its consequent over-dependence on practice, practice, and more practice for competence." He pauses. She is not sure if he is waiting for her to nod or giving her time to understand what has been said so far. She finds both unnecessary and the pause irritating drama. No, melodrama.

He resumes slowly. "I had never done any carpentering or plumbing before, but after looking through a few books and making a few mistakes," he points to the end window, which has a crack. "I put a nail through that one, it will have to be replaced—" he pauses again. "People look at the greats, for instance, Michelangelo, and say, 'The man was a *genius.*' Yes. But that's just it. The *man* was a genius. Michelangelo was, after all, only a man, just like the rest of us. What *he* can do," he emphasizes, "*I* can do. All you need is desire. True sincere desire," he looks directly at her. But she has cone to doubt this theory of the self-sufficiency of romantic passion. She has taught music, for years, and has realized that although much of what he says is true, ambition, even if it is sincere ambition of the strongest, purest kind, is not enough—ability is also required, in proportion to the task at hand.

She dutifully looks around. There certainly is sunlight in the room. But nothing else. No paint, no canvas, no easel. The room is bare.

"You haven't been doing any work?"

"Oh— This isn't where I will paint. This is where my books will go and my desk. Think tank," he summarizes, in that false tone of apologizing for a need that he really thinks is a mark of superiority.

"Oh." She had thought he was so bent on sunlight because of his painting.

"No," he explains, "my work is to be viewed under dim lighting, and so I must paint in the same conditions of light." She wonders about the symbolism of this as he leads around corners and bends, cluttered with books, piles of boxes, some clothes, and a hot plate.

As they pass a narrow door en route, he comments, "I have even installed a shower. There was no plumbing at all when I moved in, that's why the rent is low." They step into a larger (larger, not large) room which is opaque with layers of fine, white dust.

"This will be the studio." He deftly walks around objects, "I took out a wall here," and points, "that's why there is all this plaster dust around. I want to put a backdrop here, some dark cloth," he is so full of his plans, "for when I use models," he gives her a sort of respectful smile. It takes her a moment to realize that it is she he intends to honour by putting on a pedestal. But before she begins to explain that such a position could not be anything but uncomfortable, the memory of a line, three years old (no, far older), comes to her—'You are so beautiful'—his plans are for a nude. The third name already.

"... and what I want to do next is install a solid wood counter here in the middle, to this wall, put in a sink, with a swing faucet," he has become precise, an authority in this field too, she notices, "so this side will be kind of a kitchen and that side will be for my work, mixing paints, etc. Then the walls have to be redone in drywall."

Have to be? A wall is a wall. If it holds up the ceiling and keeps out the cold and the noise—what is this 'have to be' from one who preaches the necessity of living at the barest possible level of subsistence? Really was all this work necessary? Or just desirable, just his upper class 'essentials'.

"Why?" she asks.

"What?" She has disturbed.

"Why do you *have* to put up drywall?"

"You can't put thumbtacks into plaster and I have all of my prints to put up yet. I have to be surrounded with wall to wall prints," he says glowing, "van Gogh, Rembrandt ... "

'Have to be' again, from one who would criticize my teaching as selling out, as distracting from my art, to pay the 'unnecessarily' high rent (show me a house for cheaper, why do you need a whole house for yourself, show me someone who accepts tenants with a piano and a dog, well the pet is a luxury and why don't you use a piano at the conservatory or something, well there are lots and lots of prints *and* originals at the galleries and why don't you just fuck off).

"… Michelangelo." He sees the accusation in her eyes. "One's environment greatly affects one's work," he states simply, as if that settles a disagreement.

Yes, she thinks. Yours has succeeded in keeping you from it for months. But she tries to agree—not to gloss over, but to show, again, that no matter how much he would like to see in her a nonbeliever to be converted, she is already of the same order as him, that she too is an artist, one who feels greatness.

"Yes," she says, "that's why I like it where I am. I like the silence, the bush and stream in the back, the trees out every window—"

"But that's looking *out*," he attacks, "you're looking beyond, escaping your immediate environment."

She is startled and cannot reply. He is determined in his vision of her.

The guided tour is over, no hums and hahs had been forthcoming. He leads her back to where the desk was. His hand wafts to a stool for her, and they sit facing each other. She notices the yellow papers covering the desk. Pieces of the credo he is assembling. Two years ago he had said he'd send her a copy when it was finished, to explain what was too much to go into then, yet what was the basis of their fundamental differences, he had said. She does not ask if it's any nearer to completion.

He gazes at her, steadily, lengthily, hoping perhaps to achieve a mystic intermingling of eyebeams. For a while she meets his eyes, for a while she had hoped the same, but then bored, she turns away, pulls out of the staring match. She realizes he will interpret that as her inability to face, her having something to hide, her failure to pass the test of his no-exit eyes. This bothers her because it isn't true. She simply no longer accepts the romantic notion of communication by silence: such messaging is not pure, but ambiguous, in the inner ears of the beholder alone. So she speaks.

"You know, I've been thinking of the various arts. When you paint, you must conceive *and* execute. When I compose, I just conceive: as a composer, I'm not expected to perform the piece as well. I guess I wonder if that makes composers lesser artists than painters." She continues, "Sculptors are like painters but choreographers are like composers. Writers—well we all know how to write so the execution is—is that it? The degree of difficulty in the execution determines—"

"Drawing, painting, involves a large degree of skill too though. The gestures involve as much fine motor control as playing a piano—"

"Do they? I mean, if I were to be able to play my compositions, well, I'd have to be spending at least a couple hours a day at the keyboard just for maintenance, and I don't want to take that time—"

"But why not? If it is a part of your art, you must—"

"No, there are others who perform, others who have spent lifetimes with their instruments, why should I try to compete? And don't forget, I'm just talking about piano. Would, you say, then, that I must learn each instrument of the orchestra so I can *finish* my work, execute my symphony? That would be impossible."

"Well," he comments carefully, "it wouldn't be impossible. But you must do as much as you can, as best you can." She can hear him adding 'Patty'.

"Well I do." She is getting defensive again. "In fact, I just finished getting all my compositions for solo piano on tape. They're not perfect performances, but it's better than nothing ..." She trails off, hoping for praise, or at least, interest.

He winces. "Better than nothing?" He makes her feel as if she'd committed some despicable sin. "That's compromise. Why do it at all if it's not the best you can do?" She has to agree. She admired his perfectionist, uncompromising view. It struck a sympathetic chord in her. But she sighs, thinking of how she'd had to record each piece at least twenty times until she could get from beginning to end with not one wrong or missed note. Then she'd hear a crescendo not done just so or a ritardando not paced as well as she wanted. And if the expressionistic aspects were well done, damn it if she didn't just hit an f there instead of g. It was frustrating work. It took weeks during which she hadn't composed or written anything at all. She had finally finished the taping, accepting imperfect attempts as better than no attempts at all. At least now she could sit and listen to her work—it was different to listen when not playing—and to learn from it. And now others could hear it. After all, she created not just to create, but to communicate.

"Have you ever heard of Wittkower's theory of the *non finito?*" she asks. "The works of art that are never completed because execution constantly falls short of conception? Well, if I adopted your view, my art would be *non existo.*"

He doesn't laugh. "But at least then when you did compete a piece, it would be perfect. It would last. It would stand with the masters."

"Then when." Yet she has to admit that her own many compositions are pale beside his few leaping torsos and serene visages. No, she rationalizes, it's just that I am more critical of music than painting.

He pauses, sorrowfully. "You're too impatient."

"Perhaps, yes." Why does she always give in? No, it isn't exactly giving in. There is perhaps some truth to his diagnosis—mirrors can be helpful. Yet she feels defeated, corrected again. She hates the role (always diagnosee) she sinks into when with him. Other times, she would leave, now.

So why doesn't she leave? Now? Why does she keep coming back? At first, she knows, it was because he was one of the few people who was conscious, passionate, actively thinking and feeling—this attracted and stimulated her. But now, she has her own consciousness and passion and doesn't need to play parasite anymore. Now she keeps coming back because it's important that he know this. She must make him understand. That he is no Christ. And she, no disciple.

So she doesn't leave. Instead, she reaches out with her hands. "We haven't touched yet." He smiles and joins his hands with hers. There are words she doesn't say, words half-formed lying restless within her flesh: as long as I am behind you, child, beneath you, body, or above you, goddess, I am not beside you, human being. She moves her fingers across his hands—marble can be sculpted, it is given meaning by the hands of the artist who molds, interprets, creates as he desires, but you cannot create me as you wish, I am not stone. And every time you raise your chisel, another piece of my freedom to be and be taken for what I am, falls away.

"What happened there?" he asks, noticing the scraped knuckles of her one hand.

"Oh", she smiles, "I'm working on a new technique, playing with one's knuckles."

"Looks like it's working," he smiles back.

"Actually one of the strings was off and I tried to tighten the pin with just an adjustable wrench. I need a ratchet wrench of some sort, I think."

"Ah," he understands. "It's good you're trying to tune it yourself." The compliment insults. "You should learn how to repair your instrument too. You should know everything you possibly can about your instrument. The wood ..." He becomes quite intense. No, that's not right. He is never really *not* intense. "... a thorough knowledge of and excellence of materials is *essential* if one is to work with those materials to produce a piece of great value."

Upper class remnants again, she thinks. Who is going to pay for this Yamaha concert grand you say I *need*. And I have better things to do than learn how to build a piano for god's sake. One lifetime is all I have, maybe.

"Do you know what Michelangelo did?"

She nods but he doesn't see it. Or refuses to believe it.

"Some sculptors just sat in their studios and ordered their marble and they got what they got and that was that. But he, when he was ready to do the pietà, he—"

"He went to the quarry himself."

That stops him. But only for a brief moment. His eyes continue to penetrate as he carefully forms his sermon, statement by statement. "Yes. And do you know how he chose the marble?"

It was a rhetorical question, but she was ready. "He waited," she imitates his gravity, spacing her words as he does, "for the first light of day." She has interrupted, anticipated his punch line, destroyed his delivery. "I read that book too," she adds.

He recovers quickly. "Yes." He pauses. She pictures herself running through the jungle chasing ivory. "And that is why there is no marble sculpture that surpasses the pietà in excellence," he ends, reverently.

She is surprised. That causal relationship is new to her. Something about it feels wrong, but she doesn't say anything. This bothers her because she is sure he interprets her silence, again, as awe and acceptance.

A week later she realized what felt wrong. It wasn't just the causal connection that she rejected, it was also the implied premise: she didn't think the pietà *was* a great work of art. Michelangelo had sold out. For one, the piece shows the annoying and sexist stereotype of woman as mother, static support, of man, saviour, hero. But that was the conventional perception, so maybe we'll excuse that. (Though masters should rise above convention.) Further, at the time of the crucifixion, Christ was thirty-three; that would have made Mary at least forty-five, she figured, perhaps more like fifty or fifty-five. Yet the pietà shows a woman in her twenties. Clearly Michelangelo thought the ideal woman was young, perhaps even childlike.

Too, though not a nude, the pietà shows a woman who is pleasing to look at. He obviously also thought that physical beauty was important. More important than showing the feelings, the thoughts, the experiences, Mary must have gone through. The pietà has not one wrinkle to show her pain, her courage, her own heroism.

No, she is simply *young* and *beautiful*, and therefore *revered*. The three points of the female triangle. How unlike a master: Michelangelo presented and adored mere Beauty and Youth, instead of Reality and Truth; it's all outside instead of inside, all form and no content. So excellence of matter does in *no* way ensure excellence of substance.

That form is related to content is a leftover value of your upper class childhood, she thought. A value you obviously hang on to. You wander around all day mumbling 'Do I dare, do I dare' and then you pick up the circular saw (purchased, not rented or borrowed, it is a good investment you say, too aware that I know your laundromat job pays only $3.70 an hour) instead of a paint brush. You spend months installing windows—imagine my amusement when I discovered they weren't in your studio.

You're so preoccupied with the *form* of being an artist—with reading voraciously, speaking passionately, living in great faith, undergoing tests and trials. I could remind you that you have done only seven paintings—of which three are copies and two, unfinished—but you would call on Leonardo for justification, telling me that he left only thirteen, all of them great works of art.

At which point I would recite your definition of greatness: to be great is to move others to greatness. It's a tautology. It doesn't say anything. It's all form and no substance. It's empty. Like you. And all you create.   Like the pietà.

1983

When I submitted this to a journal, I was surprised to read the note accompanying their rejection letter: the main characters are clichés. I protested (to myself), 'No, they're not! Phil is real! So am I!' But with so little experience and no friends for comparison and context, I didn't realize—Phil was real and a cliché. So was I. See This is what happens *for further development of this …*

February 2021

Suspended

she sits in the third row
at the second desk
wearing one of those new shirts
with words on it—
her words are in black and blue:
all dressed up and nowhere to go.

the laws of her country won't allow her
　　ever to go back
and the laws of this country won't allow her
　　to go forward
until she looks like, speaks like, acts like,
　　thinks and feels like
us.

the first one is easy,
she has done it already.
the second two are more difficult
though she is learning in my class,
and she is trying hard.
but the last two are almost impossible—
and she cries with each cut across the grain:
she is made in Taiwan.

Crisis

"Uh—Jack? We have a problem."

"Oh hi Bill, what's up?" He switched the telephone receiver to his right hand and looked at his watch. Always hated to be bothered by problems from the floor, especially right after lunch.

"Well, it's about our new Broadcaster, we—"

"CMX-5? But the station just bought that one! It's the latest in a fine line of computer broadcasters," he quoted the specs, "with a guaranteed monotone to reflect professional objectivity and minimize audience upset."

"Yeah, I know Jack, but, uh, there's a problem, with—"

"With what, speak up Bill—"

"—with the voice, it—"

"That voice has been designed and tested for maximum appeal, in pitch and timbre—"

"I know, but—"

"And if there is a problem, you can just reprogram it—a little deeper or a little fuller or—"

"I know, I know. Listen, it's not that. It does just fine on the sports and the weather and the upcoming events, and the stock market report and the farm report, but—"

"But what? I tell you that's a perfect machine! We spent a lot of money on CMX-5—"

"It's the news, Jack."

"What news, what do you mean?"

"The news broadcast."

"What about the news broadcast?" He was losing his patience.

"Well, it started a couple hours ago, on the eleven o'clock, it kind of slowed down—"

Jack was relieved, and irritated at the incompetence of his subordinates. "Bill. The pace can also be reprogrammed. You should know that. You—"

"But it's not exactly the pace. I mean it'll read one item at the right pace, say the item about the prime minister's vacation, but then another item, that residential fire last night on Winwood Street, it'll kind of, well, not exactly slow down, but have pauses every now and then—"

"Look, please don't sound so helpless. It sounds like just a loose wire or something. I'll send a couple boys from Maintenance down first thing after break. It'll be cleared up by the two o'clock." He waited for a response.

It came, doubtfully. "Okay."

Bill was sitting on a stool in the Broadcast Room, with a small notebook and pen in his hands. He had come down every hour since the maintenance guys left, to monitor any changes in CMX-5. The two o'clock news went fine. The pauses had started again at the three o'clock, but they were hardly discernible, and no worse than before. The four and five o'clock were the same. That was encouraging—at least the problem was stabilizing. He thought he'd just check it out once more, with the six o'clock, before going home.

"Good evening, this is the six o'clock news from KBC.

"First, the weather: the high today was 6 degrees, low tonight expected to be 2 degrees, brisk southwest winds continuing up to 50 kmh, somewhat sunnier tomorrow with a high of 7 degrees, chance of precipitation 0%.

"The Lavery Committee has released its report on tourism in Canada. More than one hundred recommendations are made in the report, including that the provincial governments provide more money to support the industry of tourism.

"The RCMP announced it has laid fraud charges against the Canadian subsidiary of Inwar Corporation. They allege that Inwar used false written and oral representations to defraud the federal government."

So far so good. No pauses. Nice and flat.

"An economist at the University of Vancouver stated today that the recession in the first half of this year has been deeper than expected. Consequently, her predictions for next year, based on a computer model of the Canadian economy, have been modified. Another upturn is still to come, but the inflation rate will be as high as 12.4% and the unemployment rate 18.6%.

"Another toxic pesticide has been discovered in Lake Superior fish. According to a report by The Good Earth, a small environmental group, the pesticide, like DDT, does not break down and thus will be around for at least a decade. Their research also shows that the pesticide is carcinogenic."

Bill waited for the next item. It seemed a little slow in coming. He made a note of the pause after the bit about cancer.

"And now for our feature item. The situation in India has suddenly gone from better to worse. The cease fire was violated without warning less than an hour ago in a vicious attack on a small town   just outside the capital. An estimated two thousand   people were   killed—"

Bill was busily noting the pauses when he realized how warm he felt. He got up and walked over towards CMX-5—a wave of heat hit him about two feet from the machine. After a quick decision to risk staying with rather than leaving the malfunctioning machine, he continued to scribble his observations.

"… including all occupants of an emergency medical unit sss and the local school."

The last few words were higher in pitch, he noted. And—

"arrfg umph sss—"

Bill looked up from his notebook. What was that?

"Officials say it is unfortunate that   umph   there was a school in their target site   they emphasized that the town *had* to be attacked   umph ARRrr   umph   sss"

He waited. There was no more. Bill got up in amazement. No up-coming events, no stock market report, not even a proper sign off.

"umph   sss"   Barely audible.   "sss"

He went over to pull the plug out, to prevent a complete blow-out, but something stopped him. He couldn't, quite. He sat down, puzzled.

"Sss.   umph."

He stayed and listened to CMX-5 for a few more minutes until the strange sounds seemed to subside. Then he left.

It was eight-thirty. Bill was sitting back in his office. The ashtray on his desk was filled with butts. His fingers nervously flicked the cigarette— he had stalled long enough.

"Jack, uh, it's Bill again."

"Another problem?" Jack asked, mocking.

"Well—yeah." He hesitated.

"What is it this time?"

"Well, you know the cease fire was violated in India, they had a tiff, a little skirmish kind of, and—"

"*You* don't have to give me a news report!"

"Yes, well, you know there were 2,000 casualties, and, well, that was an item on the six o'clock and—"

"And?" He cut him off to get to the point.

"It cried Jack, I swear to god the thing cried—" he blurted. There was a silence at the other end.

"It had been pausing again, you know, like I said, all through the item, then it started to snuffle or gurgle kind of— I was there, you know, to monitor it after the maintenance guys left, and, well, it started to overheat a bit. Then all these strange chuffling sounds began, and then the voice distorted, the pitch and timbre seemed to fluctuate, and—it sounded like, well, like, it just made a mess of that item, I—" He stopped suddenly.

Jack was still silent.

"Jack? The seven and eight o'clock weren't too bad, but— The eleven o'clock—you know, that child suicide— The full story is slated for the eleven o'clock, and I—well—" his voice trailed off.

There was a pause.

"Yeah. Okay Bill. I'll call Herb and see if he can come back in to do the eleven o'clock ..."

1983

See "The Nine O'Clock News" in Particivision *and other stories for another critique of 'the news'.*

February 2021

Dance, Deflection, and the Disintegration of the Persistence of Memory

or

Why the Species will just get Worse (and Worse)

Let's you and I go out tonight.

See how she sits. High heels restrict movement and force the foot to arch in a sexual metaphor; straps suggest bondage, submission; legs are exposed by the customary dress to entice the eye to the hidden apex. Breasts push up and out into prominence, with fashionable assistance. Labia-red lips are held slightly parted. Such is this day's venus. Fly-trap.

See how he moves. Shirt is tight-fitting to reveal musculature and/or unbuttoned to display chest. Shoulder broadness is emphasized with arms held slightly away from the body in suspended akimbo. Swaggering bull-legged from side to side, he thus occupies the most space, declares ownership of the most territory.

And they dance. God, they keep on dancing. Variations on a theme.

Most of those females will continue to sit and wait until they're proposed to. Then they'll bear children and raise them, and that'll probably be that. Or, if they enter some profession, they'll be far less assertive, less aggressive, and more smiling than their male colleagues.

They will not be promoted as often. Nor will they be paid as much.

For the men, it will continue to be a symbol of status to be sexually active, even, perhaps especially, outside marriage. They will expect to be, and attempt to be, superior to all women, and to the men around them. They will compete in blue collar games and white collar games, running around addicted to becoming number one.

But we know all that. And we understand it too. Social conditioning, right? Yes, that explains some. But perhaps there's more to it than that. Biological determinism? You look at me in horror. No, genetic predisposition. You think about that. Then you double-check: you're saying that it's in my genes to sit passive and pretty through life, to have children?   Yes.

I study the Dali print, *The Persistence of Memory*. Timepieces softening in the sun's heat. Pieces of time, melting.

Eye colour, you accept. But passivity? childbearing? In your genes?

Evolutionary self-selection. I explain. Consider lizards and hawks. Now suppose we have a bunch of lizards, all different lizards—some can run quickly, some can't. Then a hawk comes in search of food. The lizards scatter for cover under rocks. Which ones survive? The ones that could run fast. *They* are the ones that propagate, not the dead ones. So what attribute is genetically passed on? Speed.

Only the survival-promoting attributes remain in the species gene pool, because the specimens with other attributes don't survive in order to pass on their genes.

Now let's consider the human. Say we have two tribes—in one, the males impregnate everything in sight, and in the other, they don't. Which tribe is going to survive and continue to reproduce itself? And which women are going to pass on gene content—the ones who bear children or the ones who don't? So, necessarily, which tendency will be passed on—the tendency to propagate or the tendency not to?

A clock drips.

But that's only part of the story. Given the drive to survive, and given no reproductive limit (biologically, the male has no gestation period, and socially, he is not responsible for care of offspring), it was good strategy for the male to maximize sexual activity—the more chances taken, the more chances there were of his genes being passed on. So to have as many women as possible, and also to have the best women possible (better to impregnate a healthy one than a sickly one), it made sense to fight and compete—winners take first choice.

And for the female, who does have a reproductive limit (biologically, she has only one chance in every nine months, assuming a pregnancy to term, and socially, she must then care for the offspring for several years), it was good strategy to invest in the best, to make it worthwhile. So it made sense to encourage competition among the men so the best specimen would indeed declare himself. And it made sense to appear attractive so that she was the one chosen by the best. And, because going in search, therefore, was unnecessary (it also wasted energy needed to successfully bear and raise the offspring), sitting and waiting made very good sense.

You are reluctant—but why is that? Why do we accept the theory for every species but our own?

Because, you blurt out, it doesn't explain *me*. Am I some kind of fluke, some odd mutant, you ask. You don't want to sit pretty and you don't want to have children, yet you're obviously from an endless line of exactly that kind of women or you wouldn't be here, therefore it must be in your genes—

Only as a predisposition, I interrupt, not as a predeterminant. Think of ball bearings on a ramp. They will follow a certain path *unless* deflected. And that is how humans differ. We can change the path. We can deflect.

You consider, then question: you're proposing genetic manipulation?

No, I'm not talking about *altering* genetic make-up. I'm suggesting *counteracting* it, *compensating* for it. But we have to know what it is before we can change it, before we can establish a social network so strong that the genetic predisposition truly is affected. It requires another perspective on the relation between nature and nurture, don't you see? We must revamp conditioning, attend to other social influences, encourage the will—

Suddenly you stop me. You remind me that you're going to self-select and deflect yourself right off the ramp. So it's all for nothing. The genes of those dancing idiots are still going to be the ones passed on—no matter how carefully we structure the social network to compensate, it's one step forward and three steps back.

In one sense, yes, 1 agree. But genetic survival refers only to quantitative measures—life or no life. What about quality? There you are, *not* sitting and waiting, *not* bearing and raising, so you have time and energy to influence, to affect. the *quality* of life. What you pass on—ideas, values, questions, answers—through writing and speaking and doing, can make some ball bearings shine a bit more. So, just as others who are off the ramp by natural death have left a trace of their *genes*, when you leave the ramp, a trace of your *endeavours* will be shining through. If genes can be deflected, then genetic heritage is no more definitive of survival than ideological heritage.

You think for a moment about the effort it requires to struggle against the current conditioning. You imagine the additional effort required to struggle against your genes. You decide you don't like this theory.

But it doesn't matter whether you like it or not. It's just that you should know what you're up against when you say to men and women, 'Change, don't be so passive, don't be so competitive!'

And all of us should know *why* we do what we do. Understanding our behaviour *will* make it easier to change it. Our accusations to the men of ego and to the women of weakness are only partly justified. We must understand that so much of what we do is just derivative, complex and subtle manifestations, of that primitive impulse to survive, to carry on dancing—an impulse without which we wouldn't be here.

I look now at the other Dali print.

But an impulse from which it is now time to deflect, through social influence and individual will, in order to create a revised modern survival impulse.

A clock begins to shake into fragments.

1983

Of Human Bondage

first they tied her legs apart. far too tight, the leather strips cut into the flesh behind her knees and around her ankles. then they tied her arms as well. she would not able to move now, not be able to buffer, ride with, escape, no matter how intense the pain. no blindfold, but flat on her back she couldn't see what they were going to do to her. until they did it. there were so many of them. were they all to have a part? when they brought her in she had caught a glimpse of the corner full of devices and gadgets. she tried to imagine them advertised in some special magazine, she tried to imagine someone ordering them out of some special catalogue. they had already forced something up her anus, further than she thought possible, she had tensed up in resistance and the penetration hurt. a lot. now someone picked up another one of the objects, something silver and shining, and moved to put it between her legs. she flinched, remembering a razor blade close to her clitoris. she began to panic again, fear gagging in her throat, she should've stayed home. then someone else she'd never seen before, another stranger, stroked the inside of her thigh. relax, it'll hurt less if you don't fight. there was an uneasy silence. what were they waiting for—the high priest, her first scream? a

man walked in then, masked, so she couldn't read the
feelings on his face. he looked at her, touched her, felt
her with satisfaction. he too picked up something from
the gleaming assortment. he stood between her legs
then, ready. okay push, he said.

1984

The Gift of Life

She sighed as she awoke, then lay looking at the ceiling. Stark, white, offering no answers. It was very quiet and still in her small house. Had been for years now. No Ned, no Peppy. She rolled over and sat on the bed, hands on either side touching, holding, perhaps gripping the edge. She looked out the window. It was not a pretty day. But then, she had come to feel comfortable with these dry grey mornings.

Her feet reached into her slippers and she went over to the mirror. She was not dismayed at what she saw. Most women had stopped putting on make-up years ago because it took so much to take it off. So the face was very familiar—it was the same in the morning as it was in the middle of the day. Though it tightened a bit in the evenings. She looked intently at the face. As she had for the past month of mornings. Still, it offered no answers. And tomorrow that face would be fifty years old.

Minutes passed before she picked up her brush. It was four years now since her husband had given. Funny how words change. She remembered when people had 'passed on' or 'passed away', but now the polite word was 'giving'. 'Dying', of course, was reserved for those earlier freak deaths which still happened occasionally. And perhaps for animals. The others talk of Peppy being dead, but she liked to think that he too, gave. Whatever the words, it had been years since either Ned or Peppy were around. And yes, she was lonely.

She fixed the pins in her hair, took the faded orange robe from the chair and put it on. It was the one Ned had given her. And the one Peppy would always curl up on if she happened to leave it on the bed. Which she often did. Still.

As she walked from her bedroom to the kitchen, she took note of the rough rug beneath her feet. She let her hand stroke against the wall as she passed by. It was important to feel everything today. She let the water trickle over her fingers as she poured a cup into the kettle for her morning cup of tea. Most people had stopped drinking tea because it dehydrated the body, but for her, it was one of a very few remaining pleasures.

Six years ago, the world had, essentially, run out of fresh water. What was left could sustain only so much life. And although most couples were already limiting themselves to two children, it became illegal then to have more. It also became illegal to own a pet. They were extravagances that could no longer be afforded.

It also became law, then, to give up your life at fifty. So the water supply could be distributed 'to maximize efficient survival of the species'. Mandatory suicide, Ned called it.

She remembered that year. 2072. Of course there were millions of people over fifty, and they all had to give. It was a holocaust. So few had been able to give voluntarily: social morality and religion never does keep up with social reality and necessity. Many were still Roman Catholic, insisting that it was indeed suicide and as such, a violation of the seventh commandment: if they committed such a mortal sin, they would surely go to hell. But, some asked, what about doing for others? The response was that love of God transcends love of humankind. The pope of course advised resistance, and then the sacred versus secular power struggle broke out. It didn't seem to occur to anyone that by *not* giving, Roman Catholics still violated God's seventh commandment: instead of killing themselves, they'd be responsible for killing others, by using water that would have supported someone else. But could that really be called killing? People had been over-eating somewhere and starving somewhere else long before '72—wasn't that the same?

And others, similarly inclined to be religious, declared that the world was meant to end and the new laws were interfering. The press had a lot of fun with that faction, pointing out that their God couldn't be too omnipotent if they were worried about human action having any effect on a divine plan.

She put a slice of bread into the toaster, opened the fridge and took out the tub of margarine. No honey, it had long been like caviar, afforded only by the very rich. She'd expected jam to become rare as well, but to her surprise, strawberries required even less water than oranges.

And then you had the ones crying for freedom and liberty. We had prided ourselves on being a democratic country and this law, of course, was seen as a totalitarian dictate taking away our liberty, our freedom of belief as well as our basic freedom to choose.

And the right to life. By '69 people had become quite vocal—and violent—with respect to the old abortion problems, and for a while in '72 many abortions had to be performed: there were couples carrying their third or even fourth child. It didn't take too long for compulsory sterilization to be legislated, but instead of solving the conflict, that intensified it: the right to life of the unconceived child was being denied. Of course many countered by claiming that the right to life was simply no longer an unconditional and inalienable right.

She took a tea bag from the box, put it into her cup, poured the boiling water over, set it onto the small table. There had been no cream for years; cows were too expensive, meat accounting for close to 30% of fresh water consumption, and the whole world had gone vegetarian. She'd tried all the cream substitutes, but decided she'd rather have her tea black.

My life *is* my own. The thought seemed sudden, but of course, it was not. So the choice to *end* it should be mine. I think I would give whether it was law or not: it's a fact of life now that we just can't go on and on until we age to death, that's a luxury of bygone days. I've had my years of life, very enjoyable and satisfying, I shouldn't begrudge another the same chance, I *should* give, I *want* to give. I *too* resent the law for taking away my freedom—my freedom to give without compulsion. But of course there must be such a law. Only a few would give voluntarily. Not enough. It seems we need to be compelled by law.

I suppose in many ways it's like the draft—when wars between countries were legal and the men and women between fifteen and forty were required to enlist, required to go, fight, kill, and be killed. What comes first, duty to self or duty to others? The conflict increased for those who had children—extensions of self and at the same time, others. Though Ned and I would have been draft dodgers. Then. We didn't believe in that kind of dying. There are different kinds. Of dying.

The clock on the wall showed that only fifteen minutes had passed since she had awakened. What if all the minutes of today pass as slowly?

But— If only I could wait a few weeks. How I would love to hold my first grandchild, just once! Just once, to look into her eyes, to hear her cry, to hold the weight of her in my arms, to feel her little fingers wrap around mine, to touch— To touch the one I'm giving for, giving to.

She began to cry, again, and abandoned her toast. Her hands pressed flat on to the table and her head moved stiffly back and forth, eyes wide in a desperate denial. She reached into the pocket of her robe and got out the kleenex. After a bit, she drank a bit of her tea.

What will two weeks matter? Oh yes, I've thought of applying for an extension. But Ellie did that and was refused. And then they came round on her fiftieth birthday just to make sure. Unfortunately, she'd decided to risk it, hoping for a premature but safe birth of her grandchild. She was arrested, and her children were fined. They're still paying out. It's such a very heavy fine, to encourage the children to feel responsible too, to assist in their parents' gift if need be. Oh, Ellie. Little Tammy is alive and healthy and— She has your smile.

Suppose I risk it anyway. Ellie always was unlucky. There have been slips in the check, sometimes someone will forget or be late— That man in the paper the other day, he was discovered to be seventy-five years old! That was quite a story, all the children rushing to see the picture, they'd never seen anyone that old except in family photo albums. And relatives don't count. To the young.

But the fine, it would be too much for Laura to bear, with the little one coming along, even with all that I can leave to her. We've never been rich. And suppose I was discovered in three or four days—there'd be the fine for nothing, I still wouldn't be able to hold—

Maybe I could get in the car, go on a little trip, elude— No. They anticipated that. There were so many checkpoints …

Her fingers started picking up the crumbs from the plate, and she absently nibbled each one before swallowing.

Surely, money is a small price to pay for principles, for personal freedoms. Perhaps, but do I have the right to those principles, those freedoms? By insisting on my freedom, I may be depriving someone else of theirs. Perhaps Laura's child, my own grandchild.

What if that someone else consented? What if I could find someone willing to give a month early? Perhaps then I could be allowed to give a month late. That sounds reasonable. It adheres to the spirit of the law, the purpose, the reason. No more water is used in the bargain. She became excited— I'll need to call a lawyer, and apply. She looked at the clock on the wall, fourteen hours to find someone! She raised her cup to finish her tea— Her hand started to tremble, badly, spilling what was left.

How could I have forgotten? Ned and I tried that. Of course we did. I agreed to give two years early so he could give two years late and we'd die together. The authorities refused permission. Something about the timing being crucial, there would be an excessive demand on the water supply for those two years that would make a difference, whether or not the demand two years after was less than allowed for.

She slumped in the chair, one hand resting limply in her lap, the other still twitching, slightly, on the table. Then she sighed and began to draw circles around the puddle of tea with her finger.

She thought of Ellie again. It's not really a question of risk. It's a question of right: *do I have a right to live?* Is freedom of choice an individual's right at all times under all circumstances?

And it's a question of responsibility. What obligation do I have to other human beings?

She fixed her gaze on some distant spot through the doorway, her eyes grey and dry. She continued to sit, motionless now, but for her face slowly beginning to tighten, and her finger tracing the circle around and around.

1984

Rerun

two nights ago I dreamed
i was in a car
spinning along a dark highway
careening from left to right
out of control
twisting and contorting
finally crashing
into screaming lights and crushing noise and bloodred pain
and a voice said
crippled for life.

last night
i was naked
plunging through a dark tunnel
careening from left to right
out of control
twisting and contorting
finally crashing
into screaming lights and crushing noise and bloodred pain
and a voice said
it's a girl.

1984

Running

At our school, cheer-leading practices were held at the same times as cross-country running practices, so you couldn't go out for both, you had to choose, one or the other. I decided, against my mother's desires, to run. And it has made a difference. To me. And to my mother.

(It's not that I'm against cheering. I like to encourage others. But not loudly from the sidelines; I prefer to cheer quietly, while running beside on the same course. This too has made a difference. To me. And to my coach.)

Because no one else showed up for practices at eight o'clock in the morning, I ran by myself—thus I grew accustomed to being alone. And, to fill the space and time, I started to examine all sorts of ideas and feelings, actions and reactions—I grew accustomed to thinking. and, as my distances increased, so did my aptitudes for solitude and for thought.

Over the years, as I continued running, I developed strength and endurance, and with these qualities came confidence: I would go out freely day and night, aware that I could probably outrun any adversary. And, as a consequence of frequently choosing to stride along unknown paths, my sense of direction improved considerably.

Eventually I realized that I had become an oddity. No, as I was no longer in my adolescence, I was now downright deviant. My mother made it clear that women weren't supposed to sweat, and when she saw me once drenched and haggard (glistening and triumphant), she was quite obviously disgusted. Or disappointed. Or both. My coach made it clear that one was not to stop to pick flowers during a race or jump two feet together in the puddles, and above all, that one was not to encourage ones opponents (fellow runners). My friends made it clear that women do not go anywhere alone: you're looking for trouble, think you're too good for us? And my colleagues and professors made it clear that women were not expected to think: at the philosophy department parties, they offered glasses of wine instead of ideological interchange.

It seemed that my running, which had created so much of what I am, was clearly antagonistic to what I was supposed to be. And the results weren't the only objectionable aspect: my reason for running was also suspect and hence, put on trial.

I run for the freedom of it: it feels so good, leaping unrestrained over miles and miles of open country. My worst nightmare is having an accident that leaves me crippled for life. But others accuse that I run to escape: they patronizingly explain how it's therapeutic, a symbolic solution to my inability to fit in, to my sex-role confusion—they say I'm evading, running away from reality.

I find their negative valuation of escape strange. I suppose it depends on what you're running from and what you're running to. It is possible to escape into freedom. I mean, if you're about to be attacked by a sabre-toothed tiger (or any other life-threatening force) and you run, no one would reprimand you for escaping instead of staying to face the situation. Then again, in a way they would: according to current attitude, you *would* be more heroic if you *did* stay and kill it, or at least (how would they know) put up a good fight. Which is all the more reason for me to run.

(Do not worry. I have strength and endurance, my sense of direction is finely tuned, I am used to being alone and I think: I will outrun my adversary.)

1984

This is the person who lived over there

this is the fire that burned the person who lived over there.

this is the explosion that started the fire that burned the person who lived over there.

this is the bomb that created the explosion that started the fire that burned the person who lived over there.

this is the missile that ejected the bomb that created the explosion that started the fire that burned the person who lived over there.

this is the system that guided the missile that ejected the bomb that created the explosion that started the fire that burned the person who lived over there.

this is the person who
designed the system that
guided the missile that ejected
the bomb that created the
explosion that started the fire
that burned the person who
lived over there.

this is the material that was
used for the part that fits
into the system that guided
the missile that ejected the
bomb that created the
explosion that started the
fire that burned the person
who lived over there.

this is the person who prepared
the material that was used for
the part that fits into the system
that guided the missile that
ejected the bomb that created
the explosion that started the
fire that burned the person who
lived over there.

this is the part that fits into
the system that guided the
missile that ejected the
bomb that created the
explosion that started the
fire that burned the person
who lived over there.

this is the person who made
the part that fits into the
system that guided the missile
that ejected the bomb that
created the explosion that
started the fire that burned the
person who lived over there.

this is the person who
operated the system that
guided the missile that ejected
the bomb that created the
explosion that started the fire
that burned the person who
lived over there.

this is the company that
employs the person who
designed the system that guided
the missile that ejected the
bomb that created the explosion
that started the fire that burned
the person who lived over there.

this is the person who owns the
company that employs the person
who designed the system that guided
the missile that ejected the bomb that
created the explosion that started the
fire that burned the person who lived
over there.

this is the company that
employs the person who
prepared the material that was
used for the part that fits into
the system that guided the
missile that ejected the bomb
that created the explosion that
started the fire that burned the
person who lived over there.

this is the person who owns the
company that employs the person
who prepared the material that was
used for the part that fits into the
system that guided the missile that
ejected the bomb that created the
explosion that started the fire that
burned the person who lived over
there.

this is the company that
employs the person who made
the part that fits into the system
that guided the missile that
ejected the bomb that created
the explosion that started the
fire that burned the person who
lived over there.

this is the person who owns the
company that employs the person
who made the part that fits into the
system that guided the missile that
ejected the bomb that created the
explosion that started the fire that
burned the person who lived over
there.

this is the order that
commanded the person who
operated the system that guided
the missile that ejected the
bomb that created the explosion
that started the fire that burned
the person who lived over there.

this is the person who issued the
order that commanded the person
who operated the system that guided
the missile that ejected the bomb that
created the explosion that started the
fire that burned the person who lived
over there.

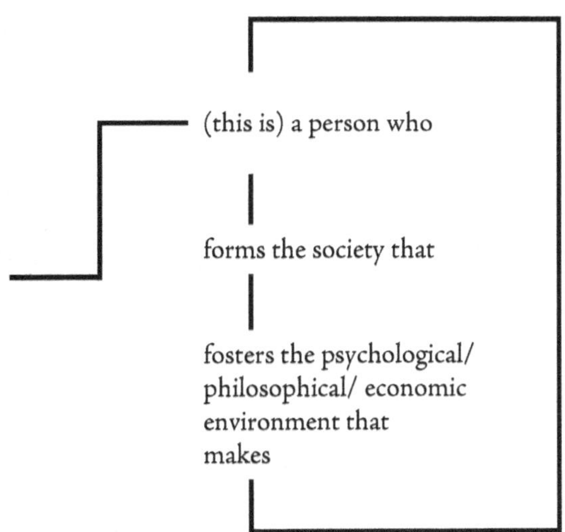

and this is the person who lived

over there.

1984

This is the person *was originally published by Ouroboros as a broadsheet (an accordion-folding poster); I still have several copies, so if anyone's interested in getting a copy, contact me!*

February 2021

Pas-de-deux

Even her foot was poised, suspended quite elegantly, almost touching the row of seats in front of them. The egg-shell straps wound around her satisfactorily sized six, which was arched out of high-heeled habit into a slight point. The line of her leg to the crossed knee was graceful, its smoothness accentuated by the pastel silk she wore, which draped in sculpted folds as she sat, still, watching the ballet. An evening purse lay in her lap, clasped loosely by two well-lotioned hands. A delicate gold chain enclosed her wrist, one strand of the several around her neck.

He sat beside her, dark leather dress shoes resting firmly on the floor. He had considered wearing a pair of fashionable pleated pants, but opted for something tighter fitting, which followed the lean cut of his legs. A simple shirt, tucked neatly into his pants, was made stylish by a thin black tie, knotted loosely around his neck.

The stage was a graveyard now. The two principals, male and female, are alone, dancing together. The pas de deux begins with splendour—she floats, he soars, extending through the air, then she holds a beautiful pose as he lifts her, caught in mid-flight, above his head—but it becomes more and more frenzied as they try to keep each other alive. It does not quite work, the passion falters and fades—another beautiful pose, he is half fallen on the ground and she is heavily collapsed over him, like Christ stumbled with the cross bearing down on his back. The scene ends—she is dead and returns to her grave, and he must leave, almost as lifeless.

The roses were presented, and the house lights came on. *Giselle* was over. The two of them rose from their seats, side-stepped behind others into the aisle and slowly made their way to the lobby. Once there he lightly touched her elbow and guided her to the lounge, where they found an empty table.

"What would you like?" he asked when the waiter came.

"A pink lady, please," she suddenly felt silly ordering her favourite drink.

"And a martini for me, please."

The waiter left. She set her purse on the edge of the table.

"So what did you think of the ballet?" he asked.

"Oh, I liked it," she said. It was the appropriate answer. But she really wasn't sure. "It was well done," she tried to amend, but realised how snobby she sounded. What did she really know of ballet—she was somewhat familiar with its poses and posturings, but she couldn't tell a Potts from a Kain.

He didn't know what to reply. Mere agreement seemed required but mediocre. And besides, he knew ballet only as a sometime spectator. "Didn't you find it a bit artificial?" he ventured. "I mean, men don't really dress like that, in those tights or leotards or whatever they're called—"

"Nor do women," she countered, bothered just then by a memory of stiff crinolines in Sunday school.

"But their behaviour too. I mean, didn't you think her approach-avoidance conflict was just a bit too exaggerated? She clearly wanted him but ran back to her mother, for pete's sake, every time he looked at her."

She fiddled with her glass before responding.

"Yeah," she then agreed, "and that ridiculous competition between the two men, one of them a prince wasn't he and ..." she trailed off seeing his look of unease.

He tried to continue, to cover, "And those solos, such blatant displays—" He stopped short, and they both sipped from their drinks. Silence for a while.

Voices from neighbouring conversations began to drift through to their table, exclamations of praise and beauty … 'Just excellent,' 'Still moves me,' 'What a classic' …

He finished his martini. "Shall we go?"

She nodded, picked up her purse, and left the pink lady unfinished.

It was such a warm night that he suggested taking a rather circuitous route back to the car.

"Okay," she agreed, and linked her arm through his.

After four blocks, she remembered that the shoes she had worn were definitely not intended for walking, and she had to ask him to slow down. After seven blocks, she wondered ruefully just what they were intended for. At that moment, he spotted a flower stand at the next corner and ran ahead to it. She watched, smiled at his impulse and tried not to ruin the gesture by approaching with a limp. She succeeded in arriving with grace, and he gallantly presented her with a rose and a kiss.

He noticed her discomfort as they continued. "Just one more block, I think."

"Good," she said with relief and offered an apology of sorts. "Perhaps the walk wasn't such a bright idea after all, I forgot I was wearing these shoes—they're not meant for walking." She tried to ignore the straps biting into a blister, and the heels whose height seemed to challenge her balance at every step.

"But they're beautiful shoes," he complimented, countered, compensated.

Five minutes later, they reached the parking lot. A thought occurred to him—he rejected it as silly—but then thought, what the hell, she's not so heavy and I've always wanted to do this. Besides, she could use the lift. Grinning, he picked her up and began to walk across the lot. She was too surprised to say anything— So instead, she put her arm around his neck. Mick Jagger. I will be your knight in shining armour.

He delivered her to the passenger side of the car, set her down, then unlocked and opened the door. She slid in thankfully, he closed the door, then went around to the driver's side.

She sat on the couch, and while waiting, picked up the booklet he had bought at the ballet, and began leafing through it. A history of the company, reviews, biographies of the dancers, and photographs.

Back at his apartment now, like a master of ceremonies, he turned on a few lights, turned off a few others, and tried to decide between Beethoven and Chopin.

He asked her what she would like, "Beethoven or Chopin?"

She smiled, impressed at the options. "Beethoven."

"At your request," he replied with a flourish and slid the record out of its sleeve and put it on the turntable.

She paused at the still of *Swan Lake*—all those ballerinas fanning out. Good thing they were all the same height. She smiled, what would they do if one of them were half a foot taller than the others? Well they just wouldn't let her in, she joked to herself.

A favourite sonata of his. He adjusted the volume then went to the counter for the wine.

He returned and held out two bottles. "Which do you prefer?"

"Oh, I don't know—" She considered the two, then pointed to the one in his right hand. "That one looks just fine," she smiled, again.

A picture drifted through her mind of a tall ballerina running from here to there trying to get into the line while all the others linked together, held tight, and refused to let her in. She looked at the photograph again. Coincidentally all of the dancers had long hair, worn in a bun. And they all had those oval faces. Not a Shirley Temple among them. Why not, she wondered. Certainly one didn't have to be such and such a height, and have such and such a face in order to be a fine dancer. Yet she had to admit to her- self that a six-foot ballerina *would* ruin the beauty of the line in *Swan Lake*. She thought back to tonight's pas- de-deux. And yes, if the dancer had looked like Shirley Temple, something would have been lost. But what? And why?

He busied himself with a corkscrew, and in a few moments poured the Chateaubriand.

He walked back toward the couch, and she set the booklet back onto the table. He handed one of the glasses to her. Then he sat down beside her and proposed a toast.

"To beauty," he said, smiled, and touched his glass with hers.

She smiled. "To beauty."

Disturbed by the dissonance between her ethic and her aesthetic, she picked up *Art throughout the Ages.* An

He glanced at the title of the booklet she'd set down. *The Classical Ballet.* Odd that it should be called Classical.

ostentatious coffee table book, she thought, but then, most were. As she leafed through the extensive photographs, prints, and illustrations, she began to notice general differences. The twentieth century architecture looked very plain and bare beside that of the baroque era which was quite decorative and ornamented. Doesn't emphasis reveal importance? Obviously utility, function, is more important, more valuable, to the twentieth century than it was to the past.

She looked at Roman and Greek sculpture. The former was very descriptive, very literal, very individual. Greek sculpture, on the other hand, conformed to an ideal, displayed 'perfect' proportions as opposed to 'real' proportions.

So the Greeks valued the universal, the ideal, and the Romans valued the individual, the real.

He'd always considered ballet to be very Romantic. So in what way was it Classical? Perhaps the form. The ballet *does* emphasize balance, line, proportion—in fact, it valued the Ideal in this respect and was therefore very Classical. But the content was definitely Romantic. The story line of *Giselle*, for instance, was practically vintage: pretty peasant girl courted by handsome duke. It presented a return to nature: the setting was pastoral, idyllic, and Giselle was even crowned queen of the harvest or something. And it seemed to rank the emotions and the senses above the intellect: the characters were certainly more passionate than contemplative. And the Classical portrays the Ideal, whereas the Romantic portrays the individual in search of the ideal. Very much like the Greek/Roman split. He wondered if the word 'Romantic' came from 'Roman'.

They happened to sip from their wine at the same time. He set his glass on the table then, and settled more comfortably on the couch. He put his arm around her shoulders to pull her closer, leaned his head back, and closed his eyes to listen to the music. She cradled her glass in her hands and looked at his face. So chiselled, she thought admiringly. She reached up to stroke it and he kissed her fingers as they crossed his lips.

It is acceptable, is it not, to judge a culture by its works of art? Can we not deduce their values, their ethic, from their aesthetic? She considered broader areas—European culture and Oriental culture. In music, the European style is generally more massive, concerned with quantities of combinations; Oriental music is very fine, displaying an economy of sound. In painting, Europeans deal with the dramatic, and use large canvasses; the Oriental artists paint on a smaller scale, and emphasize the lyric rather than the dramatic. Even poetry seemed to fit the trend: the epic belongs to the Europeans, the haiku to the Orientals. So largeness is considered good by the western world and smallness is valued by the

But what was the ideal? He recalled the 'noble savage' theme and Blake's *Songs of Innocence*—peasants and children were idealized. Certainly *Giselle* illustrated that. Not only was the main character a peasant, she was also quite the child, positively infantile over the string of pearls given to her.

And she was a woman—females were also idealized, probably because the Romantic writer was almost exclusively a male. Woman became the personification of Beauty and Purity, so the Romantic portrayed the individual man in search of the ideal women.

The Romantic desired to transcend the ordinary, the

eastern? She found it amazing how revealing art was. Truly the aesthetic did express the ethic. That which is beautiful is that which is valued, which is good, which *should* be.

"More wine?" He got up and retrieved the bottle from the counter. After refilling their glasses, he set the bottle on the table. She turned back to the booklet on dance. What ethic is behind *this* aesthetic? By seeing what was considered beautiful, she could now discover what was considered good. And she saw. The female dancers appeared to be fragile, wispy, insubstantial, weak. They had long elegant arms, and their hands seemed incapable of grabbing on to whatever it was they were forever reaching for. The toe shoes made their legs longer, sleeker—but also less able to support, and so the dancers were often in need of assistance—male assistance. Walking on pointe was like walking on tippy toe—the ballerina was like a child. And their steps had to be small, large steps are impossible on

real, and he used Woman as a vehicle to do so.

And so the individual becomes ideal, and you have the ideal pursuing the ideal.

And so you have then, the development of the Romantic types. The male, besides being, of course, dashing, handsome, and strong, must be passionate. And he must be chivalric, because if he is seeing woman as the Ideal, as Beauty and Purity Incarnate, then he must treat her with respect, with care, he must assist her at all times, be at her service.

And she, of course, must live up to that ideal. She must be beautiful, graceful, she must be delicate, soft, fragile.

pointe, and careful, to avoid injury—toe shoes restrict movement, speed. And the ballerinas often posed, static. And the male dancers? Well, they were active rather than static. They appeared to be very virile, strong, and vigorous. They performed leaps and jumps, covering much area, much territory, in breadth and height. They were very muscled. And very well endowed—amazingly so. And, of course, they supported the female, they were at her side ready to balance, catch, look after.

The types occur throughout Romanticism. Consider Keats' *Endymion*—the image of perfection is a woman; and Emily in Shelley's *Epipsychidion* ...

She set the glass she'd been holding onto the table. "Um, where is your bathroom?" she asked almost apologetically.

"Oh, end of the hall," he gestured, feeling a little uncomfortable, as if he'd been an inadequate host.

She unentwined herself from him, and headed in the direction he had indicated. Having forgotten her purse, she returned, with slight embarrassment, picked it up from the table, then turned away again. "Back in a minute," she added.

"Hope so," he said, and smiled.

But the problem was just that—they were types. Ideal types, and therefore unrealistic. In Shelley's *Alastor*, the poet is so involved in his quest for the Ideal/Woman (a peasant maid, of course, like Giselle, having fair hands and embodying truth, virtue, knowledge), that he ignores the human love of a real woman. Byron, who wrote lines such as "she walks in beauty, like the night" which go on to describe her innocence, beauty, purity, serenity, could not endure the sight of a woman eating. And Don Juan, who says "I am therefore in love … my goddess … has the voice of a lute and the song of a seraph …" is, in fact, therefore, incapable of love. As are all men who have idealized women—for an Ideal is by definition, unattainable. Furthermore, that adoration is actually *insulting*, because it is based on beauty—of form, not content—which is of the body, not the mind, which is something accidental, not intentional, something passive, not active.

He rose in agitation and walked around the room. The music had stopped and he went to the stereo to turn the record over.

The Classical ballet is an example of an entire artistic institution dedicated to perpetuating the Romantic— the Romantic *myth*. A myth which positively monopolizes adolescence and carries over, into, through adulthood: the pop songs, the movies—all show the individual passionately seeking the ideal in the other. Usually the former is male and the latter is female, but probably only because the artists is male— men probably wrote and choreographed *Giselle*—and for a male, the most obvious accessible 'other' is the female. Many, though, have chosen another other, and idealized it—they call it god. But for the most part, over and over again we are presented with Goethe's Werther: the man who turns the woman he 'loves' into some sweet angelic divinity, disallowed farts, burps, and original thoughts, puts her on

a pedestal, then laments
because she doesn't love him.

On his way back to the couch, she came back into the room. He turned to look at her, smiled a compliment, then extended his hand, an invitation to dance. She let her purse fall onto the couch, and accepted his hand. He drew her close, and she rested her arms around his shoulders. They moved together, barely dancing, swaying imperceptibly to the pulse. At each turn, his leg thrust in languor between hers, as she stepped around, encircling his thigh. They continued a while.

But of course she doesn't—
because not only has she been
denied real personhood, real
feelings and thoughts (she is
the *object* of his pursuit), but
also because *any* real
relationship between them is
impossible: it can be nothing
but artificial, so untrue to self.
Like Werther, Loys ran
around being dashing,
handsome, always at Giselle's
service, thinking she was some
kind of goddess, worshipping
her. In the pas-de-deux, he was
there to assist her, she
depended on his presence for
the poses, the turns, he helped
her balance on pointe, he
practically carried her
across the parking lot.

The differences between the
male and female dancers—it's
too bad they're so typed, but
really it's just ballet. It's just
someone's concept of 'beauty'
or 'good'—the choreographer
who designs the steps, the
auditioning committee that
selects the bodies. They make
it so the men act one way and
the women another.

But as he said in the lounge, it's
a bit unrealistic. People don't
act like that.

Yes they do. Or they try to.

They stopped dancing. She had to face the resemblance between what she saw in the ballet and what she saw around her—the big steel men, the cover girls. The types of classical ballet were no different than current sexual stereotypes. Someone's concept of 'beautiful' has determined what we, others, are conditioned to believe is good. Aesthetic *has* influenced ethic. But the more she thought about it, the less clear she became about the difference between aesthetic and ethic. In fact, it seemed there was none. They were the same. Aesthetic determined ethic but it was also the case that ethic determined aesthetic—that which is valued, thought to be good, is made into or displayed as that which is beautiful. There is indeed a relation between life and art: a circular one. What is thought to be good, in life, is portrayed as beautiful, in art. And what is portrayed as beautiful, in art, is thought to be good, in life.

Suddenly the relation between Romantic capital R and romantic small r was clear to him. They were synonymous. It was all there—the candlelight to heighten the tactile senses by decreasing dependence on sight, the wine to dull the intellect, and the paucity of verbal communication, of cognitive interchange, with the resultant abundance of emotion, expressions of passion. And the rose—symbol of Beauty, nature's beauty. The romantic moment was a moment out of time, it had no problems, no practicalities—it was an ideal, it was unreal.

They went back to sit on the couch. A bit further apart than before. She looked at the photographs again. My god, she realized, it's all false. Our standard of beauty, of good, rests on a hypocrisy, because the dancer's role is full of contradictions. She must be *very* strong (she had taken a few classes, she knew how hard it really was), but must appear weak. She must exert a great deal of effort, and often the body positioning was so unnatural— the turn out, the toe shoes, much of the practice and performance was indeed painful—but she must always smile. She must have long flowing hair, but wear it in a bun (unless she is insane, as Giselle becomes when she discovers Loys is engaged to another, or sexual, Juliet, for instance, or child, the *Nutcracker*. She must not have broad hips (it hindered correct performance of the moves), yet her costumes (the tutu) emphasized, indeed distorted the hips, as if they were

Both Romance and *romance* make men and women into something they're not—just as *Giselle* did, for it is both a Romantic ballet and a romantic ballet.

And he was therefore as ridiculous as Loys, as Werther. He couldn't deny the little things he'd been doing.

But no, he struggled to defend. instance, or a child— the *Nutcracker*). Contemporary romance is all that's left of Romanticism. It's the only testimony we have to humankind's surviving search for the ideal, pursuit of the perfect. What's dominant, even definitive of the female person.

And it's not in the repertoire to be intelligent—Giselle is, in fact, quite the idiot—so it is plain to see why I must not discuss this with him: if I did, I would be violating the ethic, the standard of good. Fool around with the ethic and you jeopardize the aesthetic. The two are connected. If I want to be intelligent, I have to forfeit being beautiful. And that's why I must accept assistance—a male opening the door for me. The aesthetic depends on the ethic—

so wrong in that?

But he knew—Byron, Shelley, Keats, Goethe—the wrong is that such a pursuit restricts the pursued, a real human being, by imposing idealistic perceptions upon it. The price we pay for letting personal relationships bear the brunt of the Romantic impulse is the depersonalization of the other, the female, as well as the disappointment and frustration of the subject, the male, when the pedestals collapse.

She recrossed her legs, and they moved closer together.

And yet, if one were to shatter the hypocrisy, act the truth, if one were reject the aesthetic, then one would also be rejecting the ethic. Conversely, to conform, to meet the aesthetic is to endorse the ethic. By subscribing to the aesthetic of this culture, my society, I am catering to the very ethic that imposes all

Rather, we should encourage each other to pursue the Ideal in other non-living entities— art, science—entities that won't be stunted, stagnated, by being put on a pedestal. And, if we must be personal about our pursuit, let us direct our focus inward, attain the ideal not through an other, but through

these contradictions, falsities,
restraints upon me.

our self.

She closed the booklet one
final time and saw the cover
shot. A foot tied with pink
ribbon in a toe shoe. Suddenly
superimposed on the cover was
a memory of a magazine
page—black leather strips
around an ankle. Then another
memory made a triple
exposure—an exhibit in a
museum, a tiny foot floating in
a jar of formaldehyde, labelled
'Adult Chinese Woman'. They
considered it beautiful. They
considered it good. She knew
how it was done: the foot was
bound, wrapped with ribbons
of gauze—certainly not black,
and probably not pink,
possibly white, but perhaps a
shade closer to eggshell.

He saw then the cover shot of
the booklet—a foot in a toe
shoe, raised, elevated on
pointe, on a little pedestal.
That's what they were,
portable pedestals, one for each
foot. She puts them on herself,
but the male certainly helps
her stay on pointe, he supports
her on pointe, she needs his
assistance to stay on pointe.

His gaze extended to her feet.
Then, to her shoes, the ones he
had called beautiful, the ones
she couldn't run in, the ones
with the high heel, that
elevated—

She reached down

He reached over

    and their hands met, embraced, joined together.

1984

My Niece's Wedding

see how they don't run
when the bridal bouquet is thrown
they walk
in the opposite direction

1984

Nocturne

Dearest Anne, I am writing to you in such misery tonight. Whether the clock has struck two or three I do not know, but there is not a half hour's light left in this poor candle stub. Becky, the little servant girl (God bless her), smuggled it up to me and I dare not go in search of another lest I be discovered. For I fear then they will take away my piano forever—

Oh Anne, what a state has befallen me! I am locked in a garret with strict orders not to be disturbed. Disturbed! As if external stillness could calm this raging fury! But then the good doctors don't account for that. I believe they don't think it can exist, they don't think anything can exist inside of a woman, they think we are all beautiful empty shells waiting to be filled with their dreams and desires— But I do run on. Surely you will soon agree that I am quite mad—and you mustn't! Anne, you must believe me when I tell you I am of clear, lucid mind as I write to you this blackest of nights.

But let me go back, in an orderly fashion. You recall when we last had the pleasure of a visit. I had come to see Mr. Liszt to request a copy of the Field nocturnes. Of course he wouldn't see me, so I left the request with his man. It was never answered. Then quite a while later, Lord Ashbury—what a name, have you ever considered it? ash and bury—Lord Ashbury gallantly presented me with the complete edition. He thought he was doing me such a pretty favour—which he was—and expected my gratitude and rapt attention in return. But it irked me that he, who knows nothing about music, should have his request attended to, while I had been virtually ignored. (And besides, the man is such an irritation.)

Indeed, one day he laughed so heartily—I didn't realize he had come into the parlour, I was concentrating on my finger crossings—he laughed when he saw me stumbling over and over crossing finger three over four and two. With much condescension he announced that finger two crosses over finger one, as if I had got it all confused and backward. Well. I stood up, slammed the piano shut, and said maybe his fingers couldn't cross three over, but mine, well prepared by hours of petit-pointe could and would! And they shall, sister, they must, if I am to play this new nocturne of mine as it must be played!

But I am so tired. Not because of these late nights spent writing, nor because of the hours of concentrated practice, but because of the bickering and fighting just to be excused from garden parties, and afternoon strolls, and yes, petit-pointe, so I can work on my art. That is what is so exhausting. Oh how I wish I could spend more time—I need more time!—but, well, you know mother. She is *so* upset with the time already spent practising, she tells me over and over I can play well enough, and certainly Lord Ashbury is delighted. Well enough for whom, I demand, I do not want to delight Lord Ashbury or any other Lord! But they cannot understand. When I do play for guests, she criticizes me for not being a gracious host because I refuse to play their requests (but do you know what they ask for?) and she thinks it perfectly insulting when I play on and on oblivious of their presence, their polite applause, or when I suddenly stop in the middle of a piece to make a note of something I hadn't realized before— In short, my intensity is embarrassing.

But back to Field. His nocturnes *are* beautiful—but in a pretty sort of way—really they are such stunted silly little things. But I suppose he can't be faulted for that (even though he studied with Clementi, played before Haydn—oh what I'd give for chances like that!)—for what does *he* know of the night? For him, it is a time of rest, a time of serenity and peace of mind, a time of semi-consciousness. But *we* know the night.

The night—the *real* night—belongs to women. Profit, power, and idle curiosity are the fathers of invention, but necessity—necessity is the *mother* of invention. It is no accident that the person to first discover that tallow on a string could burn, could give light to the night, was a woman. No accident at all. For it is in the night that our sentence of self-sacrifice (if we be wives and mothers) and artifice (if we are not) is suspended: it is a time to put down our irons and pots, our smiles and hairpins, and take up the work close to our souls. The night is vitalizing— *It is vital!* Our minds are not anaesthetized, but bursting forth in full consciousness, in searing awareness! Oh, it is beautiful and peaceful, yes, but in a fiery bright kind of way, and the stillness is that of a roaring silence!

But all of this brings me no nearer to my miserable state of confinement. Let me go on. You may have heard that Liszt's latest 'friend' is a young man from Poland, named Chopin. And perhaps you were aware of the concert he arranged featuring himself (of course) and this Chopin. (He would never consider befriending me—he will never arrange a concert introducing *me* to society—though he knows I'm good enough, and though, God knows, I've tried to make his acquaintance—his fancy is caught instead by some young foreigner.) Well of course I had to go to the concert. After all, if Liszt is sponsoring him, he must be good. In fact, he studied at the conservatory in Warsaw (another chance I'll never have). Even if he is not good, one always learns something from others to further one's own work. And these concerts are my only chance to meet other musicians (though I know the only reason I am allowed to attend is because mother sees concerts as social events not musical events—and she knows that people like lord Ashbury will be there—all of which irritates me because I know I will be treated not as a fellow musician but as a social fixture). But quite apart from all of that, it has been said that Chopin has picked up where Field left off—which of course interests me greatly.

I must write in haste now, so I shall not tell you who was there, what they were wearing, and what the talk was about—besides, that bores both of us and of course it's not at all important. What is important is what happened.

Anne, I'm not sure what came over me, but near the end of the concert I began to cry. The music was so beautiful— This Chopin, he can write— If I could have heard these pieces, studied them but a few months ago, I would've been saved much time in my own development— He can write— But then I thought, *so can I.* And there I was, a mere spectator in the audience while I knew so well that my place should be up there at the keyboard. I started to shake and I could not stop. Chopin *has* gone beyond Field, but only a little of the way. There is so much further to go, and *my* nocturnes will never be heard. Neither Liszt nor anyone else will ever take me seriously—they find women charming, and that's it. Charming! No one would call Chopin's nocturnes charming! Oh no, they call them passionate! But he doesn't know what the word means! Let them listen to me! Do they really know what a nocturne is? A nocturne is restless beauty, it is melancholy and depression of the darkest kind, it is the very soul of the night! Like Field, Chopin's chords are not broken, they are merely taken apart and presented one note at a time— But a broken chord, Anne, a really broken chord must *sound* broken, it must sound *wounded*— It must lie there on the staff in pieces.

Then of course there was an awful fuss over me, people fretting about, making much ado. When they went to loosen my stays, lest I faint, well you can imagine the shock dear mother got when she discovered I wasn't wearing a corset—'in a public place, you should be ashamed of yourself!' I haven't worn a corset in months and months, why you can't play a piano if every time you lean forward, it bites into you, and of course they all think I'm some sort of hussy now. They all think a great many things now. Some maintain I was simply moved by the sensitivity of the music—I expect Chopin loves that one. Liszt, of course, just declared it the frailty of women and suggested we be allowed to attend only the few pieces immediately preceding the cakes and ices— which sent me into another rage. Some of the women, if you can believe this, claim I was upset because Liszt introduced Chopin to Aurore (you surely remember Mme. Dudevant) and not to me.

But of course, the final diagnosis was that I was suffering from hysteria. The doctor prescribed total rest and total isolation. Which brings me to how I am now, to how I've always been, to how I probably always shall be— Raging in the black night, my candle sputtering, totally confined.

love, Amelia

1985

This became the script for a performance piece titled "Amelia's Nocturne": a monologue woven with music (piano and voice, live or pre-recorded) to be performed on a simple set consisting of a writing table with an inkwell and note paper. The scores and mp3 are available at chriswind.com.

February 2021

The Apple

(to Eve, the first teacher)

thinking about the apple
left on my desk,
wondering about the origins
of the tradition,
i suddenly remember you
and think, why of course,
you picked it from that tree,
its our symbol of knowledge.

well if its that
and not a symbol of
disobedience or idle curiosity or evil
why, i wonder for the hundredth time,
do men still condemn us?

especially since you offered the apple to Adam
you shared your knowledge with him
and he turned around
and kept it
from us
in a thousand different ways.

yet here i am
still holding out my hand and smiling
sill sharing that gift, that power,
that knowledge
(but every time a male student
walks into my classroom
i shudder
and think
   why should i?)

1986

Chastity

stripped of all pretense
you stand naked
except for the cast-iron chastity belt
clamped around your bruised and bloodied hips
rusting from urine and menses

the pain of infection and abrasion
winces in your walk

but that is nothing
to the scream in your eyes
that have seen
wired through the padlock
a price tag

1986

i was going to write a poem about
a woman who beats up her would-be-rapist
(she's been taking aerobics classes and is,
like most of these women,
in far better shape than the average man;
she's also been taking self-defense classes
so she has now the skill and confidence
to use that fitness)

anyway, i was going to write this poem about
a woman who beats up her would-be-rapist
then first aids him
(she's been taking that class too)

but i can't.

1986

Adam's Apple

i see you in the library
wandering through the HQ stacks
you stop here a moment, and there,
taking books from the shelf
leafing through
The Scold's Bridle ... Salem ...
Grace Hopper ... Rosalind Franklin ...

you stand there
nervously gulping
and it bobs up and down
something caught in your throat
some knowledge you just can't swallow.

i want to turn away
in impatience, frustration, disgust, defeat—
but you stand there still
it becomes a lump in your throat
and as tears begin to form
i think maybe
if you keep trying
you will get it down

before you choke on it.

1986

Jarrett

She breezed into the room, wearing bright red coveralls, the sleeves rolled to mid-forearm, and white canvas basketball boots, unlaced. Her left hand was in her pocket, and her right hung relaxed at her side, loosely holding her trumpet. She gave the impression of arriving fresh from Mario Andretti's track crew. Or a skydiving flight.

Her steps slowed as she neared the centre of the room, and once there, she stopped to look around her in amazement. The room was huge. The ceiling was so high, and the windows so long, so tall. And all this space. She turned full circle slowly, a smile of wonder playing on her face.

She opened her audition with Chuck Mangione's "Feels So Good". The first three notes, clear, and beautifully unrushed, didn't break the silence, but, rather, slipped into it. As the song progressed, she filled that silence, that space, more and more. And more— The pace picked up and she was moving all over the room, dancing to the music, glorying in the resonance, feeling *so* good … sometimes supplementing the off-accents with a hip or a shoulder, or walking jauntily to the beat, or swinging her entire body upward with a surging note. She played toward the end, moving less, as if to set up for a cadenza, then she stopped, profiled in the centre at the end of the room, and arched back for that grand penultimate phrase. In the break that followed, she straightened, turned to face the adjudicators, then delivered the last phrase, with stunning simplicity.

Then, only then, did she speak, to introduce her second selection as an original composition. She walked over to one of the large cathedral windows and vaulted up to sit on the window seat, one leg stretched out along the length of the ledge, the other bent up to her chest. She was silhouetted by the sun that was just beginning to come through. Her piece was a very sad, very beautiful, elegy.

When it was over, for a brief moment she rested her trumpet on her leg and looked out the window. Then she nimbly leaped down and walked over to the sound equipment. She took a cassette from one of her pockets and put it in the player. It was a 'music minus one' recording of Haydn's Concerto in E flat for trumpet. Jarrett took a central position nearer to the adjudicators' table and standing quite motionless, played the concerto through, from beginning to end.

Dr. Martens applauded. Wildly. The others just stared. Jarrett stood there, nodded a thank you to Dr. Martens, and waited. Suddenly, recovering routine, Dr. Barton spoke to her.

"Uh—thank you," he looked at his list, "Jarrett Reid. Uh—we'll be in touch."

She nodded again and walked toward the door.

When she had left, there seemed to be a collective sigh at the table, with the exception of Dr. Martens, who was still smiling, delighted.

"Well," Dr. Barton said.

"Oh dear," Dr. Whitely murmured. Then, "We forgot to do the interview with her."

"Oh—" For a moment, Dr. Barton moved as if to call her back, but that would be awkward. He hesitated, wondering what to do.

"Do we need to?" Dr. Martens asked. The others looked surprised. "I mean, 'Why does she want to study music?' She loves it, isn't it obvious?" They looked alarmed, a little uncomfortable.

"But—"

"There *are* other questions," Dr. Elderson reminded him, "testing her knowledge and—"

"You have her high school transcript, what were her music marks?"

"A. A-. A." Dr. Whitely scanned the sheet.

"All *right* then. Besides, didn't that composition of hers indicate any 'knowledge of music' to you? And her interpretation of Haydn was well-informed."

The others nodded, hesitantly.

"But— Chuck Mangione?" one said.

"And her technique?" another said.

"Look, I'm not the brass expert here," Dr. Martens said, "but I know a good sound when I hear it. Dr. Peira, how was the Haydn?"

"Good," he said. Then added almost reluctantly, "Very good."

"Well then?"

"But— She's—" Dr. Barton floundered. "I mean do you think there's a place for her here at our faculty? We have room for 125 new students and 500 have applied. We have to be selective *beyond* skill and knowledge. Will she fit in here? *That's* the question."

There was a silence.

"She's so ... different," one of them muttered lamely.

"So?" Dr. Martens asked.

Dr. Barton resumed, "We haven't room to take chances on students who won't fit in, Alex. The students who won't make it, the ones who will drop out, or fail, or get married, or change majors ... How's her background, can she afford to stay with us for four years?"

"What?" Dr. Martens asked incredulously.

"Look, I know it's unfair to have to consider these things, but we have face facts, we're a business as well as an educational institution. You read the Dean's report, this faculty cannot survive if third and fourth year enrollment isn't as high as first year. We have to be sure the ones we admit will continue."

Dr. Martens sprang out of his chair and went to the window. The others restlessly played with pens, papers. After a moment, he wheeled around, gesturing in exasperation.

"Why didn't we consider these factors with the hundred who have preceded her?" He paused and folded his arms. "What have you got against this one, this Jarrett Reid?" he asked.

There was another silence.

"Well, she's such a—a *performer*," Dr. Elderson ventured.

"This was a *performance* audition! Look, you admit she has the skill, she has the knowledge, she *certainly* has the spirit or 'musicianship'—"

"But Alex, she's so different, it's just we're not used to, didn't expect …" Dr. Whitely trailed off.

"I move we hand in our ballots," Dr. Peira said.

Each of them finished up their adjudicator's report, then submitted their ballot. Dr. Barton tallied their evaluations. Three to two. Jarrett Reid was admitted to the faculty of music for her first year. She had passed.

The class was loud, as usual, but rowdier, more restless. It was mid-term time, and anxiety, and activity, levels were at a high. Today was her turn for the exam in Conducting 101: she was to lead the class through the rehearsal of a piece—she was to conduct. Dr. Martens took a seat at the back.

Jarrett put two folios of music under her arm and stepped onto the podium. She looked out at the class and waited for their attention. It was not forthcoming. She set the music on her stand and raised a hand. Still no change. She stood there then, shoved her hands into the pockets of her jeans and waited.

Eventually, gradually, the talk decreased, slowed, stopped. Eventually they were looking at her.

She smiled, "So. What'll it be: Beethoven's *Sixth* or Louie's *Songs of Paradise?*" Conversations were resumed almost immediately. Again she waited for a bit, hoping they were discussing their options, then she raised her hand, again. Silence was once more slow in coming, and she decided to interrupt.

"Shall we take a vote then?" She fought against shouting.

"You're the conductor, you're supposed to decide!" A student called out over the lessened but still continuing talk.

"Yes, I am the conductor, but that doesn't mean I'm a commander too." By now, most were quiet. She explained, "I didn't think there'd be any point in working through a piece no one wants to play—"

"Let's go with Alexina," the voice called out, singsonging the name.

"Nah, too weird, I vote for the Beethoven."

"Bor-ing."

She waited again until there was enough quiet to take a vote. A count of hands showed Louie to be in favour. She handed out the music amid increasing flurry: adjusting music on stands, tuning instruments, wetting reeds, then warm-up scales and arpeggios.

"Jack, you'll need a bow," Jarrett called out to the percussion player. "I didn't think any of our string players would be willing to lend you theirs," she grinned, "so I brought an extra. It's by my desk."

She waited until all the strings had put on their mutes, then when she began to hear fragments of the first section, she tried to begin.

"Okay," she fought against shouting again, "we don't have a tam-tam, and Bob, since you'll be required on the vibraphone, I think we'll just leave it out rather than try a substitution, okay?"

"Okay," he said after a pause. Surprised when he realized it wasn't a rhetorical question.

"Now there's a time change after the first two bars, from four-four to three-four, so let's try just the first four bars. I'll count you in one bar." She had to wait a long time for silence before she could give the upbeat. Half of the strings were a beat late entering bar four, still counting in four. There was no reason for the error, especially if they had been watching her.

She looked at the string section. "We need more unison on the crescendo and decrescendo, bars two and four, and watch the metre change." She paused. "Let's try it from the beginning and go on this time."

She stopped them at section B. It had been dismal indeed.

She smiled playfully, "So how do you like it so far?" Few smiled back.

"Look, at bar five there's a *rit*. Watch me, I'll keep you altogether, 'cuz at bar six we have to change speed, suddenly, '*subito* quarter note at 72,' as opposed to the opening, quarter note around 50. Then at B, the score indicates 'getting faster little by little'—at C we have to be at 88. Now I know we'll be nowhere near that since this is just a first playthrough, but we can certainly capture a change in pace, right? Let's try it again."

A general buzz followed her comments. Eventually they were ready. They got to E this time. Well, most of them. Again, the performance was much worse than it could've been, than it should've been.

"What's the problem with the metre? These are my patterns." She demonstrated two-four, three-four, four-four, and five-four with her baton. "Okay?" No response.

She tried to compensate then, "Great try, Steven. That oboe part is rather intricate, eh? And the balance is good, everyone, sounds good," she added lamely.

They struggled through sections of the piece again and again.

Suddenly the first violinist interrupted. "Excuse me," he called out in the middle of a section.

"Yes?" Jarrett asked.

"Bar fifty-five, when I enter with the solo, I seem to disagree with your dynamic indications. I'm entering *mf* crescendoing to *f*, and you seem to want me to enter at *mp* or *p* even. This is a solo. It's supposed to stand out."

Jarrett looked at her score. "Well, the initial dynamic isn't indicated. So maybe you're right, but even at *p* you do stand out, because only one other person is playing at your moment of entry. All we hear is a single flute tone—"

"But starting at *p* is just too weak, too unobtrusive."

"But this is a subtle piece. I think it shimmers rather than glares. Besides, starting at *mf* doesn't give you much room to expand, and the peak is clearly marked just *f* not *ff*." He seemed not to have heard her last comment. He was talking to the violinist beside him.

A few other musicians then had questions, comments. After a while, they were ready to play again. At several points, too many people got lost and they had to start again somewhere.

Jarrett tried to make a few of the *fermatas* over rests inordinately long, an attempt to use silence as a timbre, but the attempt was lost. No one was with her: they all paused the usual extra 1.2 seconds, by conventional consensus, and went on more or less together.

Eventually the class was over.

Dr. Martens left the classroom and went directly to his office. He sat down at his desk and went over the notes he had made during Jarrett's conducting. Oh she knew her hand signals, they were very clear, and visible, she never confused functions of the right and the left hand, her cues were always ready and necessary, her tempo metronomic, her understanding of the piece impressive, in fact it was quite a commendable choice, Louie was not only contemporary, and Canadian, but a challenge to *any* conductor for the frequent changes in metre and the precise dynamic indications—but, well, *Jarrett* hadn't conducted the piece, the orchestra had conducted themselves: when it came right down to it, her presence hadn't made any difference, as a conductor she had not succeeded, and he felt he could not award a passing grade. She had failed.

It was December, a week to go until Christmas break, and the end of the first semester. Student conferences were held during this week. Jarrett arrived for her 2:00 appointment with her advisor, Dr. Martens. She knocked on his office door, and heard him call out, "Come in."

She opened the door, and walked in. "Hi."

"Hi Jarrett, have a seat."

"Thanks." She sat down.

"So how's it going?"

"Well …" she smiled and settled deeper into the chair, stretching out and crossing her legs in front of her. She put her hands in her pockets, then began to answer his question. "Normally, I'm not too concerned with marks. I'm here to learn about music and sometimes the marks reflect what I've learned and sometimes they don't. It really doesn't matter to me. But *since* I'm here, and *since* you asked," she smiled mischievously, "well, it matters to the university. My marks, I mean."

"Yes?"

"You know I got kicked out of ensemble."

"No. I didn't know. Why?"

"'An excessive number of flagrant violations of the dress code.'" She grinned.

So did he. "But wasn't it explained to you? There's a reason for the dress code."

"Oh yeah," she paraphrased, "'A concert is not a visual event. Music is to be heard and not seen.' So any non-uniform attire and/or colour disturbs that; the eye distracts from the ear. But if it's just an aural affair, why doesn't everyone just stay home and listen to their stereo systems?" She paused. "And I move too much. I detract, I upstage the others, I stand out."

"And what did you say to that one?"

"That if *everyone* moved, I wouldn't stand out."

He laughed.

"I know what they're getting at," she rushed on then, "I go to concerts and I see what they want. But I *hate* what I see. Everyone in the audience is sitting in their best dress, stiff and still. Like statues. No one dares to move. Not even to Strauss. Ditto the orchestra. Only soloists are expected, allowed, to move. Orchestras have always looked to me like a crowd that wandered in from a funeral. Deadpan faces in black suits and ties. I tell you if *I* were the composer—"

She corrected herself, "—*when* I compose," then carried on with excitement, "I'm going to specify: this symphony is to be performed *con moto, literally,* by people in colours. All sorts of colours. Music is played with the body, it's an affair of the heart, not the head. I wonder if it's just a coincidence that most of the people in music are men, and men are notoriously inept at expressing their emotions. Sometimes I think that's how we've gotten to where we are: sober, except for the soloists, and even then, the emotional spectrum consists of 'intense' and 'more intense'. Seldom joy, celebration ..."

She continued to ramble over ideas and impressions, as if they were boulders on an oceanside hike. "Maybe it's just men in groups. Then again, no, look at any all-male pop, rock, or jazz group: *they* move, it's clear *those* people *feel* the music they're playing. So maybe it's just 'serious' music. Hm, the name itself— Maybe something happens to people who *study* music, people in academia— I mean, they're the ones who eventually form the orchestras, right? Maybe something ... maybe I should get out while—" She stopped then, a bit self-consciously.

"No, I don't think you should get out," Dr. Martens finally had to say something. But then couldn't say any more at the moment.

She resumed then, with less animation. "I may not have a choice. That zero in ensemble isn't going to help my average any. You know that first year students must have a B average in all their music courses to get into second year, to stay in music I mean. And a B+ in the course they want to major in."

"Yes … "

"The mark you gave me in Conducting. It's not too helpful for my average either. Or as my major prerequisite."

Dr. Martens raised his eyebrows. He hadn't realized until now that she wanted to major in conducting, that she intended to become a conductor. It pleased him: in addition to having a special, superior, understanding of music, which he felt she, of all his students had, a conductor had to express the music physically, visually— He recalled her audition. She'd be perfect!

Jarrett continued, or rather ended then. "It isn't a fair mark. I think I deserve a passing grade in Conducting." She sprang up then and looked out the window, uncomfortable with sitting so long. And saying so much.

"I see," he paused, his mind racing to recall his reasons for the failure. She hadn't been perfect, she …

She turned to him then. "Can we talk about it? I mean, why did you think so poorly of my conducting?"

"Well," he started slowly, "for starters, you didn't have the attention of your orchestra. A conductor must have attention to do a good job of it. Perhaps you could've clapped your hands, or asked them to be quiet—"

"Clap my hands? *Ask* them? No one else had to. My presence on the podium should've been enough. It's standard courtesy to be quiet when the conductor ascends the podium," she gestured slightly as she spoke, as if conducting her words.

"Yes, I know." He paused, then tried again to put his finger on her problem. "Perhaps it was your voice, not loud enough to get their attention."

"But that's it. I shouldn't have to *get* their attention, I should *have* their attention, I'm the conductor. You pay attention to your conductor, any musician knows that."

"Yes, but your conductor is in control. From the start it was clear you weren't. You let *them* make decisions, instead of making them yourself. The first thing you said was 'Which one do you want to play, Beethoven or Louie?'" He paused. "What would you have done if they had chosen the Beethoven?"

"Nothing different. I was prepared for both."

He smiled. She would be.

"But that's not the point." She sat down restlessly, then leaned forward. "Don't you think that a group that has a say about what it does performs better? Why not approach it as a collaboration, it really *is* a group effort, isn't it? There's no point in playing something no one wants to play. It'll never sound good. And that's my responsibility as a conductor, to make the music sound good, right?"

"Right, but then when the soloist interrupted you to quarrel about your dynamics, you let him!" Now Dr. Martens rose to walk around the room.

"Well what's wrong with that?" She turned in her chair.

"Never ever let a *member of the orchestra* interrupt *you—you're* the conductor!"

"But I'm not infallible, or omniscient. He knows the violin better than I do—at least he should, it's his instrument. He may have had a valid point. I'm open to comments, suggestions. Just maybe someone from the orchestra will make a suggestion that I've never thought of before, a suggestion that will change the piece, that will make it closer to what it was intended to be. Two heads are better than one. Thirty or fifty are fantastic!"

"But not when you have a job to do. Not when you're trying to lead them through a rehearsal."

"When then? My job is to bring out the best possible performance of the music and—"

"But you didn't do that. What you got was a very muddled, pathetic performance." He paused, sat down, and tried again. "Perhaps it was something else in your style … It was so … Unauthoritative. You smile too much."

"What's wrong with smiling? Why should I be mean and militant? Is that the only style people pay attention to?"

"Well, maybe!" He shrugged his shoulders in frustration. He knew *he* didn't conduct that way. "Look, Jarrett, they didn't pay attention to you, they didn't listen to you. I don't know why. But none of the other students so far have had that problem, so it must be something you did or didn't do, can't you see that?"

"Yes. All right, you're right. It *was* the things I did. What I did *was* different. But being different is no reason for failure."

"But the others can conduct. Their way works. Your way doesn't."

"For now, it doesn't, and only because it *is* different, because it's not what they're used to. Their way works because we've been conditioned to follow that way. Response to that which is different has always been reservation and reluctance at the least, rejection and rebellion at the extreme. Surely you know that."

"Yes," he nodded, remembering again her audition, the heated interchange among the adjudicators afterward. Yes.

They were both silent then.

"But I wonder if that's just part of it. Perhaps there's more to it than what I did or didn't do." She sounded back by the ocean, picking her way over rocks and roots. "I've always thought, like you, that *I* was the problem. My differentness. I thought it was individual. But more and more I'm wondering— It's too bad there aren't other women in the class. I mean, haven't you noticed that all the other students are guys? Men? So what I mean is okay maybe it is just me. And maybe a guy like me, I mean acting like me, conducting like me, would have the same problems. But maybe— There are many—" she paused for the word, "eccentric conductors who are quite successful. *Male* conductors. So I wonder if part of the problem is *that*. I'm not male. And maybe that in itself explains why they responded to me like they did. Why they didn't automatically pay attention, why the soloist challenged my interpretation. Or maybe because I'm not a man, I do things differently, maybe other women conductors would act the same, different way. In either case, the end result would be just what we got, right?"

"Right ..." he was following her trail.

"I mean, when you stop to think about it, our society does not condition people to pay attention to women. We're not in the habit of seeing women as figures of authority, in positions of power—"

"'Wait till your father gets home'" Dr. Martens smiled.

"What?" she stopped, then found his path. "Yeah. I was thinking of times when I'll say something, and no one will comment, and then some guy in the group will say more or less the same thing and then everyone responds to it. Geez that bugs me. It seems women and/or women's ways are just not listened to."

"So you're saying you couldn't help but fail up there on the podium?" he queried.

"Well, I'm not sure. I'm just saying maybe it has less to do with what I did or said or didn't do or didn't say than with the fact that they're simply not used to a woman conducting. Tell me, how many of the conductors you've worked with have been female?"

He didn't have to say it. None.

"So it'll take some time for them to adjust, accept, realize that I deserve their attention. It seems women have to earn respect. You men just ... get it. Just because you're male."

Dr. Martens didn't answer.

She grinned then. "I don't usually talk this much. And if all I wanted was a good mark, well I would've done it differently. I mean, I would've conducted the same as everyone else. But I didn't. And unfortunately, the mark does matter a bit. And the mark you gave me seems unfair. I know how to conduct, and you know I do. You marked me on how well the orchestra followed and somehow I feel I can't possibly be responsible for that, and yet …" she continued before he could object, "and yet, you are correct in saying that when it came right down to it, the orchestra conducted themselves, I didn't conduct.

"But," she was back on the beach, with the waves crashing in, "I'm starting to see that every identity requires co-operation. Maybe that's hard for you to see because probably most of what you have tried to be has been accepted, recognized. So you haven't known that what you are depends on the other's behaviour as much as your own: a leader isn't a leader unless someone agrees to follow him, a teacher can't be called a teacher if no one consents to be his student. Likewise, until someone chooses to recognize me and pay attention to my behaviour up on the podium, I am not a conductor. All I'm asking is for you to wait until that someone does. And it'll have to be soon, if they keep seeing me up there—*then* evaluate my conducting ability."

He sat silent for a while. "I suppose what you're saying … In this case, yes, it does seem that your success, my evaluation of your success, is somewhat dependent upon what other people do or don't do." He paused, thinking. "But I can't change the mark I gave you. Or, let's be honest, I won't." He went on quickly then, "But there are many more conducting assignments during second semester. You'll be on the podium twice a month instead of once. So they'll have to get used to you." He smiled, then said seriously, "At least, I hope they do. But," he continued with a sigh, "if they don't—I mean, if another semester isn't long enough—remember that half of the exam is written, and there are several written assignments from now until April." He paused. "And," and smiled, "I would consider extra work, for marks."

She smiled then too. "Well. I can't ask any more of you." She rose and reached out to shake his hand. "Thank you."

Dr. Martens stood to meet her hand. "Thank you," he said quietly.

It was spring, fresh and bright outside. Inside corners were still dull with too much study, too little sleep, and the stress of final exams, but most students were finished, or almost finished, with their year.

Jarrett noticed Dr. Martens' door open, as she sauntered down the hall on her way out. She stopped a moment and swung partly into his office. "Have a good summer, Dr. Martens."

"Thank you, I will. See you in the fall," he looked up as she moved on.

"Yes, you will," she called back.

"Oh, Jarrett, " he got up quickly and went to the door. She stopped then. "What have you got planned for your summer?"

"Oh," she leaned against the door frame and crossed her feet. "You know those street-corner musicians … "

"Yes! You're going to play your trumpet in the open air, you're going to be a summer minstrel!" He was pleased. "Good practice. And a little money too."

"Well, no, actually," she grinned. "I was going to be a street-corner conductor."

He looked puzzled.

"I thought I'd take a whole bunch of music on tape, set up a small cassette player, then conduct it! A bright t-shirt, a crazy pair of pants, and Stravinsky—that's all I need!" She laughed then, at his expression. "Good practice, don't you think?" She waved and moved on.

Was she kidding? He returned to his desk.

A second later she reappeared at his door. He looked up, questioningly.

"If I left my baton case open, do you think anyone …"

The first (and only) story in an abandoned collection of 'first year' stories; I'd intended to write about a young woman in her first year majoring in Philosophy, as well as a first year law story, and a first year of medicine story … but I thought I'd be saying the same things over and over. Besides, things looking promising with L. A. Law—*but then* Ally McBeal *seemed a step backwards. Yes, there's been* Commander in Chief *and* Madame Secretary, *but they seem to be exceptions. Besides, that's just tv. As for the real world, take a look at the website* What is it like to be a woman in philosophy? (beingawomaninphilosophy.wordpress.com) *and remember the Montreal Massacre …*

February 2021

Miami Vice
and the Roadrunner

you say its a sign of health
(Maslow, hierarchy of needs)
that a society like ours
is concerned about violence on tv
    there are real people being tortured
    in a thousand interrogation centres

so i say its a sign of sickness.

1987

The Thought

philosopher's stone, this
this figure, this man
sitting chin in hand
all heavy, and solid,
and symbol:

no one dares disturb
his thought
his furrowed brow—
     rather, we wait
     for wisdom
     for transformation—

        he considers
     and reconsiders,   he imagines
               he reflects,
       he deliberates,   meditates
      he thinks
        about

what to have for breakfast.

1987

Boot Camp at the Arcade

every day after school
the troops march in

i can hear the sound effects
as cheap a trick
as the laugh track on the sitcom
sandwiching the news

over and over
again and again
aggression violence injury destruction
    without motive
    without consequence

(oh but it's not the real thing)

(no—
for the real thing
they use high definition screens)

1992

The Middle East Theatre

the cast is a cattle call
the script is sophomoric
the direction questionable
and the tickets are way too expensive
so hell no I won't go.

besides
i never did like charades.

1992

like a whale
caught
in a concrete cage
whose voice
hits surfaces so hard
so impenetrable
it rebounds and echoes
into a cacophony
perhaps unintelligible
certainly ineffectual

and one to the nth
is the loneliest number

like that whale
I choose now
to be mute.

1992

Can she bake a cherry pie?

(wondering about U Soe Myint's torturer)

i sprinkle flour onto the oversized cutting board
and plop the pastry in the centre
it is cool, a bit clammy
the colour of unhealthy skin
it is a mound
but it lies before me
like a leg.

i sprinkle flour on the rolling pin
it is my mother's
large, solid
and heavy as an iron bar.

i begin my job
rolling forward and backward
forward and backward
pressing down, from my shoulders, hard
forward and backward
careful to keep the pressure even
forward and backward
forward and backward
it is tedious work
forward and backward

the pastry thins
forward forward
forward and backward
forward and backward

a translucent spot suddenly
        splits into a hole
and i gasp
at the bone
breaking through

i cry

(no, Billy boy, i cannot.)

1992

U Soe Myint spent over 29 years in a Burmese prison as a political prisoner, subjected to various tortures, including the rolling of an iron bar up and down his shins until the flesh was broken.

February 2021

The Lamp of Learning

I used to burn with passion
I thought I'd light the way
but I was a woman with knowledge
and a female teacher is an oxymoron
(unless she's maternal or flirtatious or simply exceptional)
so I was a witch
I was a martyr
(I thought I was exceptional)

You torched me
with non-cooperation, simple and without malice
perhaps experimental, perhaps habitual
you torched me
with a FUCK OFF!
flung like the book
that barely missed my head

You torched me
with a lack of support
a warning or suspension or dismissal
for—for whatever reason was convenient

You torched me by inflating my marks
so my judgment didn't count
so I didn't count

well—
You have siphoned
the last drop of vital fluid:
the immolation is complete
and nothing remains of me
but this burnt black bit of wick.

                                                            1993

Hendrix at Monterey

what an awful sound
NOMELODYNORHYTHMJUSTTHIS
DEAFENINGWALLOFFEEDBACK
he lays it on the stage
and kneels over it
(an act of blessing? of worship?)
he thrusts upon it and comes
(like a very bad Nijinsky)
squirting gasoline from cock height
he sets it afire
then hits it bashes it against the floor the speakers
until it's in pieces

so. let me get this straight:
he plays it
he honours it
he fucks it
then he kills it.

and he is idolized.

(what an awful sound)

1993

Isadoras of the Sky

'The Women's Air Force Pilots (WASPS) was a special unit formed to free up male fliers for combat duty during WWII. The women were assigned to ferry military planes of all types all over the U.S. and to help train male combat pilots. One of the training exercises involved towing long cloth sleeves behind their planes so the bombers' gunners could practise with live ammunition.'[1] Not to mention live targets.

the shooting gallery at the fair:
aiming at those flat metal cut-outs
ping! and it springs over backwards

one better, skeet-shooting:
pull! and a clay pigeon
flings into the air
pow! and it drops

better yet, WASPS doing aerobatics:
from time to time
we missed
the sleeve
and got the plane

oops.

in memory of the women who died this way

but i guess it was either them or you
i mean, how long would you last in combat
without practice to make perfect
your killing abilities?
(and Uncle Sam needed you, is that it?)
(or is it that you were a husband, a son—)

yeah we didn't have computer simulations
back then.
okay we did have special cameras,
we could've used them instead,
but hey,
there's nothing like the real thing, baby

so why weren't they permitted to shoot back?

besides no one forced them into the planes
and hell, we were the ones
gonna be sent into combat
so don't whine to me about
who's so easily dispensable

and the men who killed them

"*I hope what we did somehow helped pave the way for the women of today, who now can fly in combat.*" Ain't that a privilege worth dying for. "*I hope people remember us.*"[2] Oh yes, we will.

---

[1] paraphrased from an article in the *Star Tribune*, Minneapolis

[2] Elizabeth Wall Strohfus, WASP

1993

Final Jeopardy

Women's Studies for 400, please.
Answer: Secretaries in France, doctors in Russia,
    kindergarten teachers in Canada, and
    heavy labourers in Bali
    have these two things in common. Sarah?
What are the female sex,
and a job considered unimportant?
Yes, that is correct!

Labour History for 200, please.
Answer: Before women entered the paid workforce,
    this job had high status and high pay. Sarah?
What is a bank teller?
Right you are again!

Political Science for 600, please.
Oh, there's our daily double!
How much would you like to place?
Four thousand, please.
You're betting everything you have?
Yes.
All right, here it is:

The strategy that calls for
    women all over the world to become
    excellent soldiers. Sarah?

What is the best way to end war?

                                                        1993

While i was in the hospital
recovering from several gunshot wounds
hoping i wouldn't be one of
this week's eighty-three dead
victims of political violence
i watched tv—
and saw the important news break
interrupt *Dallas*:
fifty-eight had died during
the week of riots in L.A.
shock was duly registered
and amplified worldwide
everyone was aghast
and i wondered
fingering my blood-soaked bandages—
When a black South African dies,
does anyone hear it?

1993

to be or not to be:
that is *not* the question
if you are a man.

if you are a man
the question is
to do or not to do.

being and doing
pink and blue

mauve.
(do be do be do)

1996

Nero's Song

Quarter after. Plenty of time, unless there's seven staircases, no service elevator, and a floorplan designed by a bunch of Vengeful White Rats. I park my car at the front entrance of the hotel and walk in. The wedding reception for Smith and Jones? Yes, it's in Room B. Room B. In the older hotels, it was 'The Cloud Room' or 'The Grand Ballroom'—what has happened to imagination? Yes, Room B is up one flight, best access is through the side door. I repark my car and begin unloading.

Wait, 'The Grand Ballroom' is imaginative? I guess my baseline has moved. Because kids today, they can't think, their interior terrain is, well—the colour of hospital bedsheets. The justification for teaching history used to be that if you don't remember the past, you're compelled to repeat it. But even if you do remember it, you're compelled to repeat it, unless you can imagine something different, can you spell 'alternative'? (No, not P-e-a-r-l-J-a-m.) It's because people can more easily imagine a nuclear war (or several—as if one wouldn't be enough) than a revolution against violence, worldwide disarmament, a whole planet that just says no …

I used to be a high school teacher. But the stuff that goes on, the stuff that *doesn't* go on—well I quit, or was fired, or was suspended—I don't remember, there were so many schools, so many stupidities. Talk about an inability to think, a failure of imagination, an absence of alternatives. Talk about Dan Quayle.

Any school is as good as its administrators—and, well, its metal detectors. Not its teachers, not its students, not its Ministry guidelines: any teacher can use the guidelines to teach the students what's really important. But any teacher who does that will be fired by the principal before his or her probationary period is up. (And any teacher who doesn't isn't likely to start after two years.) It stands to reason: Who wants to be a principal? Not Sidney Poitier. Try Tony Danza. And we think most highly of the people who are most like us, so who's going to get hired and offered a permanent contract? Not the teacher who explains how to put on a condom, not the teacher who refuses to stand for the prayer, not the teacher who insists that failing grades appear on report cards.

So I got a job on maintenance at a camp. Pretty safe, I thought. It turned out to be a rich kids' camp, which might've been a problem, especially if I was the one who was supposed to lead the 'Merger Maniac' game. ("'Pro bono' is so Greek for 'tax shelter', just say yes, you little robber-baron-wannabe.) But I wasn't: I was the one who was supposed to repair the dock, fix the door, cut the grass. I figured I could handle it, integrity intact—even cleaning the toilets. It was a waste of my abilities, yes, but someone had to do it.

And the world is full of wasted abilities, do you think for a minute that every science graduate has been fortunate enough to get a job doing science? And all economics majors are now economists? Half of us knew a university degree wasn't job training. (The other half was in Business.) What we didn't know was that we wouldn't even be able to use our skills in the non-job areas of our lives. If you have an education degree and you try to teach someone something but you're not in a classroom in a school, then you're accused of (and resented for) trying to teach them something! Accused! (Actually, now that I think of it, you're resented for trying to do that *in* the classroom too.) And psych majors are 'always trying to psychoanalyze everything!' Whenever I use my philosophy skills, I'm accused of 'being picky' or I'm dismissed as 'an armchair philosopher'. If I had a *job* in philosophy, if I had an office in a university, then it would be okay. Then I'd be 'a desk philosopher', I guess. The importance of furniture.

Anyway, back at the camp, I eventually noticed that the cleaning products I was supposed to use were relatively toxic. My rubber gloves disintegrated. (It's the little things, you know?) So I put in an order for environmentally-safe products. And I made a fuss about the styrofoam plates and cups being used: not only did I have to eat there and so contribute to the ozone depletion, I also collected the garbage— hundreds and hundreds of styrofoam plates and cups each day. I got them recycling all the pop cans too. Things were going fine. Until I was the one who was supposed to split the wood for their campfires. Well. I heat my cabin with a woodstove, so I'm not unfamiliar with the task. But for campfires? Trees are an endangered species—one that happens to help us breathe—so I'll certainly not be the butcher when they've been killed for recreational purposes only.

Being a disc jockey is okay though. The duties of a disc jockey are not inconsistent with the deontology of hedonism—to party is to fulfil the pursuit of happiness. The perk is that this can be done without violating my other prime directive—do not hurt anyone. (Spock would be proud.) (But can you picture him partying?) So it's okay.   Except for the wedding receptions. I have trouble with those.

If only the facts weren't so bad: one in four wives is severely beaten during the course of her marriage; almost sixty percent of the women murdered in Canada are killed by their husbands; and yet, this is what hurts, ninety-four percent of all women get married. Only ninety-two percent of all lemmings go over the cliff.

So I feel like one of the players in the orchestra providing accompaniment to the Jews being marched to the cattle cars. And I am waiting for a woman, one of these nights, to spit on me. What will I say? Will I too insist that my performing here, now, does not condone, it's not that at all, no, I abhor what's going on, but all I can do is give this last gift of beauty to you, this last bit of fun ... The other gigs—the retirement parties, the bowling banquets, the funeral bashes—they're okay.

It's ten to nine. I'm all set up with time to spare. I begin cuing some of the songs. Like the first song. We're often asked for suggestions. During training, one guy suggested "The Bitch is Back." Everyone laughed. Everyone *also* laughed when another guy messed up a practice run and introduced the newlywed couple as Jim and Shaun. I mean, make up your mind.

Often the bride has a list of requests ready—including, especially, the first dance. Why does the *bride* usually do this? Because women are more sentimental? But I've never seen it as a sentimental thing, it's more of a symbolic thing. Men try to dismiss it as sentimental, i.e., emotional, i.e., not properly their realm. Yeah right. Like men aren't emotional. Ever been to a Jays' game? Maybe the truth is that men are incapable of symbolic thought. But no, that's not it: they have symbols too—the finger, the fist— Ah, it's the gendering of emotions: some emotions are pink and some emotions are blue.

Back to the first song. The Carpenters have had it. And fifteen years ago I might've suggested Rod Stewart's "Tonight's the Night," but I don't think people know anymore what the bride's wearing *white* is supposed to symbolize. (It's the colour of surrender, of relinquishing power.) "Dream Come True" was fashionable for a while, but Frozen Ghost seems a bit passé now. If pressed, I usually suggest Peabo Bryson and Roberta Flack's "Tonight I Celebrate My Love (For You)." One, it's a duet (albeit a heterosexual one); two, it states the only grounds upon which I can accepts weddings: I can't accept them as a matrimonial party, matrimony as a legal contract or as a religious ceremony, but I can accept them as a celebration of love. The key word is 'tonight'.

It's nine o'clock, they're ready to begin. I always do a short introduction, more to get everyone's attention than anything, so I pick up my mike, introduce myself, and ask them to form a circle if they like, for the first dance, with or without their cameras. Unlike the students in most of my classes, they listen to me, and do as I've suggested. This always catches me by surprise.

After the first song, which tonight was Bryan Adams' "(Everything I Do) I Do It For You", I usually play something a little bit faster, to get everyone onto the floor. Not too fast though—men are more apt to dance if they have a woman to hang on to, and therefore don't have to move anything but their feet, in that complicated step-together step-together step-together pattern and women are more apt to dance if a man dances with them. I choose Stevie Wonder's "I Just Called To Say I Love You". It was either that or Engelbert Humperdinck's "Please Release Me (Let Me Go)". ("For I don't love you anymore …")

As I begin to line up the next set—I think in sets of five or six, all in a similar style, say 50s and 60s or rock or country, but differently paced, say one slow, two mid, one fast—I see the bride approaching my table. I used to dread being asked to play "Daddy's Little Girl" for the traditional father/bride dance, until I decided that it was less immoral to lie and say I don't have that one than to go ahead and play it. Eventually I did the Nixon thing and said it had been taped over so I didn't have to lie. She asks, however, if I have any Glenn Miller to play for her parents. Sure, I tell her, no problem, and I pick out "In the Mood".

It's interesting. Women almost always ask if I can play such-and-such. So do men—most of the time. But every now and then I'll get one who *tells* me. Tells me 'People aren't dancing to this stuff!' (as if I hadn't noticed) or tells me Play such-and-such!' (forgetting that I already played such-and-such and no one danced to it either.) They tell me how to do my job. Because of course they know; more than that, they know better; what am I saying, hell, Father knows best. It's only advice though. Given with a smile. They're only trying to help. So it's hard to tell them to fuck off. (Not too hard though.) I recall a friend, explaining her lesbianism, asking me 'but don't you find men, all men, just so, so *arrogant?*' I hadn't been able to name it then. It *is* arrogance. It's also naïveté.

But what's worse, and more typical, is that the women always ask from the other side of my table, perhaps leaning over to meet my lean; so many men come right up around the table to stand beside me. It's so pathetic, their need to seem in control. It's also dangerous. And, as it happens, it's also unfortunate because I usually forget what song they ask for.

On the other hand—on the one hand, it's the other hand, but on the other hand, it's the same hand—only the men ever ask if I'd like some help carrying the equipment; the women never do. And yes, I accept their help (the stuff weighs 250 pounds altogether, I weighed it one tired night), but I ask first if they're sober and strong—being male is not enough. Hey, that could be an advertising slogan—for IQ tests …

It's time for the bouquet and the garter. This is the worst. I wish I could stand out in the hall like I used to when the anthem was played before the morning announcements—doing my Debbie-the-cheer-leader-on-speed imitation. But I'm supposed to run the rituals here, I'm supposed to promote the propaganda.

"All right, the bride is going to throw her bouquet now. So all you single women out there— Run away! Run away!" But seriously, I do wish once, more than once, that no one would get up onto the floor. Or they would, but then they'd simply step back as soon as the bouquet was thrown. But that'll never happen. Why not? Can't they imagine that alternative? Is it so unthinkable? Or is it that they just haven't stopped to think about it at all. Do they lead such unexamined lives? No—not necessarily—there's something else: a photo in the family album, me lunging to catch my sister's bouquet— I was eighteen and I *had* thought about it, had already decided I was not going to get married and yet, I got onto the floor. I didn't make a scene. I did as expected.

And now, fifteen years later, not quite still, but certainly again, I'm about to do—as expected. And, since I'm not naïve about it, I'm pathetic. And dangerous. But I'm also imaginative: surely there's someone here, some would-be principal—

"It's time for the bouquet and garter—do we have a volunteer to be Master of Ceremony for these, these incredible anachronisms?" There.

Integrity intact. The best man lurches up to my table. I give him the mike and simply step back. Washing my hands.

"All right, all you luscious available babes—onto the floor!" He laughs and takes a swig of his beer. "And Marie, are you out there? Got your bouquet? Oh that's pretty." The crowd loves it. "Now I'm gonna count to three—" "Think you can?" The guests laugh at this challenge from the floor. "Who said that? 'Course I can. Ready? Okay. Here we go. Ready? Are you ready? Okay. No, wait." He waves the mike. "I'm gonna count backwards, okay?" Applause. "Ready? Okay? Here we go. Three—two—one!" Consider it a hand grenade. Someone catches it. More applause. It must have a delayed detonator. That's always the way. The guy hands the mike back to me.

So now it's time for the garter. I just don't understand the garter thing. I mean, exactly what expression is the bride supposed to wear? Why don't we put the bouquet down the groom's pants for the bride to reach in, grope around a bit to some jeering and leering before pulling it out, triumphant as the crowd cheers? I solicit the guests again and a bridesmaid in yellow chiffon, Brutus, steps forward.

I'm so glad the 'money dance' is going out of style. It's on my checklist to ask about, but of course I don't. To ask would be to imply an expectation. For those of you who don't know, the money dance is when one by one each man at the wedding reception dances with the bride for a short time, after contributing a bit of silver. It reminds me of the old dance hall where girls could work and the men would pay, what, fifty cents a dance? And the kissing booth at the country fair. And red light districts. I wonder if the groom stands at the side collecting. He may as well just haul her off to a room and let everyone have a go at her. I mean, let's do away with the decorations.

The garter's off, a feather now in some man's cap, a trophy later hanging from his rear view mirror. I start the next set. This crowd seems divided between big band, 50s and 60s, and pop/rock, so I'm having a great time. I don't get into country and western much, and I hate doing the Guns and Roses crowd, but tonight I'm dancing a lot, really enjoying myself. "Walk Like A Man" puts a grin on my face—I always imagine a parade of gay men in drag strutting by. And Dion's "The Wanderer" takes me way back to rollerskating at Bingeman's Park, I can feel the wind in my hair. And "Unchained Melody"—what can I say—quite simply, it enchants me. And then there's a new one, "Superman's Song", that I quite like—partly because I love the cello, and the guy has a Tom Waits sort of voice—but also because it examines something we've emulated, something we've taken for granted.

However, lest you think that what I do is completely trivial, and bereft of *any* social and political import, let me say no, there are possibilities. For instance, I just played the Stones' "I Can't Get No Satisfaction" and followed it with their "You Can't Always Get What You Want". See? I can make a statement. Another fun sequence is Escape Club's "I'll Be There", followed by Grapes of Wrath's "I Am Here", and then UB40's "Here I Am", finished off with Blue Rodeo's "What Am I Doing Here?"

And being a disc jockey is a bit like being a newspaper reporter (another short-lived career of mine) (for all the same reasons): merely by choosing what to include and what not to include, you're making a statement, a value judgement. I cannot, I do not, play Bobby McFerrin's "Don't Worry, Be Happy". And I can and I do play Alice Cooper's new one, "Hey Stoopid".

Soon it will be time for the last dance. The guests will form an arch or whatever to congratulate the newlyweds. (I've never understood congratulating someone on getting married, or getting pregnant: I mean congratulations are for *laudable* achievements, laudable *achievements*; we would not congratulate someone for something for which they can take no credit—having blue eyes, for example; having sex is not much of an achievement and any idiot can get married.) And to wish them into happy-ever-after land. I consider cuing Aaron Neville's version of "Everybody Plays The Fool". But I compromise and decide to play Dionne Warwick's "That's What Friends Are For"—which was, note, written for a benefit for people with a fatal disease.

Remember that I said that sometimes I feel like one of the members of the orchestra accompanying the Jews to the cattle cars? More often, I feel like Nero playing his fiddle while Rome burns.

I didn't start the fire and I've even tried to help put it out. But it hasn't done any good. That time I got a recycling program going at the camp? After I left, all the pop cans that had been collected went to the dump anyway. And they said they'd look into an alternative to styrofoam dishes, but paper—*not* the alternative I had in mind—was too expensive. And all that stuff in the schools? I got threatened with dismissal for teaching the students how to put on a condom. Now they're in the washrooms for god's sake. And for refusing to stand for the prayer, I was 'severely disciplined'. Now it's been declared unconstitutional. And after introducing recycling into a Family Studies unit, a negative report went into my file and the course outline remained unchanged. Now Environmental Studies is a course on its own. I'm happy with the changes, but *my* actions had absolutely no impact. While others have been thanked, applauded, and honoured with awards for 'innovative' and 'responsible' teaching, I've been reprimanded, suspended, and fired.

"Rebel Without A Clue"—the title of my autobiography. Maybe I should've focused on legislative change. But when I got fired for inappropriate attire (grey cotton pants and a pink sweatshirt), I did eventually write to the Minister of Education (my own MP doesn't feel obligated to speak for me, he speaks for his party) seeking to change the clause in The Education Act that justified the principal's decision (the principal has the right to set the tone of the school and relevance to education need not be proven). The Minister thought the clause was okay as it was and that was that.

Maybe I should've gotten media coverage. Well, actually I did with the professional attire issue. To no avail.

Maybe I should've garnered the support of others. I mean maybe if I'd polled the teachers, I would've found that the majority agreed with me and would also refuse to stand for the prayer. But I doubt it. They wanted to keep their jobs. And maybe if I talked to the other workers at the camp, I might've found some others who didn't want to support the use of styrofoam. But most of them just gave me weird looks whenever I 'got all philosophical'.

Maybe, maybe. Maybe the ones who succeed just get lucky, maybe it's all a matter of chance.

And the odds are pretty bleak. They're the colour of hospital bedsheets. Most people don't like change: they're pinballs taking the path of least resistance, the path that's expected. Furthermore, they resent anyone who suggests an alternative. What, the way we've been doing it isn't good enough for you?

So fuck it. Why should I worry? Why not be happy? I put on "Footloose" and dance like crazy. With my fiddle.

1997

on watching a man
toss his empty bait container
into an ice fishing hole:

do you think all holes
are for garbage?

trash cans,
    sink drains,
        toilets,
            vaginas

1998

Masculinity Kills

this is for the sixteen-year-old boy
a daredeveil debutante
whose body flipped over his Evel Knievel bike and
snapped like a twig

this is for all the suits
corporate climbers
who fell thirty stories off the ladder
when the coronary hit

and this is for every man the military made –
they were right:
there's no life

2007